ArtEZ Press / VP

REDEFINING MUSICAL IDENTITIES
Reorientations at the waning of Modernism

FOR THEIR SUPPORT OF THIS
PROJECT, WE THANK

Amsterdam School for Cultural Analysis
ArtEZ Hogeschool voor de Kunsten
Fonds voor Amateurkunst en Podiumkunsten
SNS Reaal Fonds
Universiteit van Amsterdam

TABLE OF CONTENTS

INTRODUCTION

The authors of this volume attempt to come to grips with the
changing position of music in society and culture. The 20th
century witnessed a depth and breadth of developments in the
arts as has never before occurred in history. The producers of
art and its consumers have come to occupy separate spheres.
Traditionally, the production of art had always been dependent
on commissions and on the public. Around 1900 production
began to precede any interest of potential commissioners,
spectators and audiences. In music, this gap was even
wider than in the visual arts: it took only a few decades for
museums to catch up with the cubists, the surrealists, and
all the other painters who renounced traditional depiction
based on the rules of central perspective. But the composers
who challenged the rules of the musical equivalent of central
perspective, 'central tonality', suffered a different fate. Even
today, a symphony orchestra with too much Schoenberg or
Webern on its programmes may not attract enough listeners
to fill a concert hall. Should that be reason enough to restrict
the audience's diet to Bach, Mozart and Mahler? Almost all
music professionals will resist such a conclusion. So will
any government agency responsible for the promotion of the
creation and diffusion of artistic products. But here we face a
paradox: political decisions on the funding of orchestras may
well be dependant on the immediate attractiveness of their
programmes to the audience. Any political demands for a fixed
quota of new music on programmes thus creates a tension
between introducing 'new' music to concert audiences (and
the epithet *neue Musik* continues to be used now and again for
music dating to before World War II) and the very conditions
of survival of the musical body required to bring the new
music to life.
 At the beginning of the 21st century the situation seems, in
some significant respects, to be different from the situation one
hundred years ago. Today no clearly identifiable avant-garde
is breaking the rules (which rules are still left to be broken?)

in order to develop new styles (which styles have recently been established?). How will the music history of the future describe compositions created in the present decade?

We are even confronted with what we might call a musical 'retro-garde': composers who reach back beyond the innovations of old-fashioned modernism, and revive forms of tonality rather than elaborate on dodecaphony and serialism. Some of these composers reject the Vienna School outright: 'Schoenberg was for me the filthy, rotten dirt damp of the 20th century.'[1]

1 John Tavener,
*The Music of Silence,
a composer's testament*,
New York, 1999, p. 14.

The first contributions of this volume deal with modernism and its critical reassessment. 'Exile of Modernism' is based on an interview with composer Klaas de Vries, taking as its departure a quotation from Milan Kundera's novel *Ignorance*. De Vries emphasises the obsolescence of the issue of *traditionalism* versus *modernism*. He believes that we are exiles of a time when this issue was still of importance, comparable to the way in which the exile from Kundera's *Ignorance* relates to his country of origin. In his view, there are no more true modernists. Instead of attending to past issues, one should address advancing populism and the insidious infringements of commercialism. These are threats to the values which are essential to European musical culture: a concern with nuance and authenticity in listening and composing. They have created the problem of *non-listening* and jeopardize a more adventurous music programming for concert series. Although it is hard to convince the present-day generation of politicians of its relevance, De Vries believes that the composer has an obligation to promote auditive receptivity, in order to open people's minds to musical discernment and to new listening experiences.

Musicologist and philosopher Albert van der Schoot discusses the issue of musical innovation within a wider historical perspective. He approaches the 'music of the future' from the perspective of *Wirkungsgeschichte*, starting from the thesis that our process of understanding the present is informed by the past, while at the same time that very past today is understood from our present perspective. He analyses several instances of the 'music of the future of the past': music of the 14th century (Ars Nova vs. Ars antiqua), the latter part of the 16th century (the Florentine *Camerata*; *seconda prattica* vs. *prima prattica*), Wagner ('the Artwork of the future') and Schoenberg (atonality vs. tonality). In each of these instances theoretical positions preceded or accompanied the actual development of compositorial practice, and each had a decisive influence on the future course of music history. The 'imaginary museum of musical works', now cultivated in the concert hall, is the result of a living history in which composers deliberately chose from various alternatives. Van der Schoot advises concert-goers to listen to each composition as a developing *forma formans* rather than a completed *forma formata*.

Roger Scruton, who is best known as a philosopher but who is a composer too and the author of a widely read book on musical aesthetics,[2] conceives of *rhythm* as the inner life of music. He compares two ways in which rhythm is incorporated into a musical composition. It can be added to a piece of music 'from outside' (e.g. a beat produced by a drum-kit), or it is an organic part of the music itself. In this sense Scruton contrasts the indifferent sound-complexes produced by Stockhausen and his followers with the living rhythm in Messiaen's *Turangalila Symphony*, in which the barline 'is the effect, and not the cause, of the rhythmical order'. The example of John Adams's 'Short Ride in a Fast Machine' exemplifies the effect of De Vries's problem of *non-listening*: influenced by an increasingly dominant exposure to the ostinato rhythms of pop-music, composer and audience alike have accepted the 'tyranny of the bar-line' as a 'benign dictatorship', satisfying our basic needs.

A second group of contributions deal with music in its socio-cultural and its spiritual context.

Composer Leo Samama, former artistic director of the Residentie Orkest of The Hague, can serve as a poignant illustration of the paradox mentioned above: his city council compelled him to introduce new music to his programmes *and* to attract new audiences, recent immigrants included. The future funding of the Orchestra depended on his results in reaching these targets. But potentially new audiences do not particularly care for new music, and requests for more money are not particularly popular with the city council…. Nevertheless, the Residentie Orkest has shown great ingenuity in serving a multi-cultural community. This classical symphony orchestra has succeeded in attracting new target groups, for instance when 1,700 of the city's young Turkish inhabitants attended a performance of both contemporary serious Turkish music and Turkish popular music.

Peter Davison, artistic consultant to The Bridgewater Hall, Manchester and the editor of an earlier volume dealing with developments in music after Modernism,[3] discusses the role of the concert hall as a spiritual centre of the community. He refers to Nietzsche's 'post-religious' philosophy in order to emphasize that music 'transfigures a region in whose chords of delight dissonance as well as the terrible image of the world charmingly fade away'.[4] This amounts to a renewed emancipation of music as a transformative and binding force in society: a new turn after a post-war period when the spiritual life was out of fashion, and its connection with cultural life was systematically severed. The decay of traditional religion enhances the 'transformational' value of music, and Davison claims that the concert hall, such as his Bridgewater Hall, may be the new *temenos*, replacing the

2 Roger Scruton, *The Aesthetics of Music*, Oxford 1997.

3 Peter Davison (ed.), *Reviving the Muse: Essays on Music After Modernism*, London 2001.

4 Friedrich Nietzsche, *The Birth of Tragedy*, ch. 25.

sacred space of ancient temples, providing a core of inner stillness as the prerequisite of authentic spiritual experience. Davison believes that the concert hall has an iconic status as a public building, signalling to the people that they belong to a community through the communal experience of great music. Musicologist Sander van Maas, on the other hand, contends that the religious element has never really been excised from Western musical practice, not even during the post-World War II music revolution. Following on from Messiaen's denial of the reality of a divide between sacred and profane music, he calls for a reconsideration of *the limits of the secular* in terms that reach beyond traditional dichotomies. He ascribes the apparent absence of the religious to its neglect by those reflective disciplines that address music: aesthetics, music theory and musicology. Messiaen himself declared that he composed music in order to 'illuminate the theological truths of the Catholic faith'; he believed his music to be capable, by means of a synaesthetic mixture of sound and colour, of bringing the listener to a state of *éblouissement* or 'dazzlement', described as 'a breakthrough towards the beyond, towards the invisible and unspeakable'.[5] Referring to authors as Derrida, Marion and Nancy, Nietzsche's successors in 'post-secular' philosophy, Van Maas pleads for a reconsideration of the revelatory potential of music.

The third part of this volume deals with traditional roots for compositorial innovation.

Composer David Matthews focuses on Benjamin Britten (whose assistant he was at Aldeburgh) and on Michael Tippett. He was convinced by these two composers of the continuing validity of tonality and of traditional forms as the symphony and the string quartet. Matthews supports their insistence on the duty of the composer to play an active part in society as communicator, approaching the audience instead of staying aloof from it as is the modernist's attitude. As in many compositions by Stravinsky and Bartók, their music relates to the tradition of folk music. Can such works still be written in the cultural climate of today? The author calls for a renewal of the musical tradition through a tonality which includes essential devices such as modulation, a properly functioning bass line, and dissonance as a disruptive force. He gives several examples from his own work, in which he stresses the importance of dance and song, and of the classical sonata form, and the concept of development in particular, as an inexhaustible archetype, and finally counterpoint as an essential means to enhancing the expressivity of one's music. Musicologist and composer Rokus de Groot observes that for centuries 'oriental' musical identities, generally connected to religious or spiritual concepts, have been constructed in Western music. During the 17th through early 19th centuries these articulations were often related to geo-political and

5 Olivier Messiaen, *Conférence de Notre-Dame*, Paris 1978.

religious tensions between Europe and the Ottoman world. Religion functioned as an obvious distinguishing characteristic in the definition of cultural identity. During the general secularisation of the 19th and 20th centuries orientalist musico-religious constructions played an ever increasing part in the spiritual reorientation within Western societies. Paradoxically, oriental missionaries, while adhering to a heteronomous concept of music, could relate to their Western publics by means of the privileged position of absolute music among the arts in Europe. Western composers in their turn apply Eastern musical and spiritual sources in devising music as a spiritual exercise. De Groot shows 'conversion' to be a major theme in the multitudinous musical constructions of the relationships between the Orient and the Occident.

Oboist and biologist Borislav Cicovacki discusses new music in the context of Serbia, both historically as part of the former Yugoslavia, and in its present-day setting as a nation in its own right. Several historical factors are analysed: Serbia's former cultural marginality; the late introduction of innovations from the music of 20th century Europe; World War II and the triumph of communism in Yugoslavia; the political and musical gap between Western and Eastern Europe after World War II; the Balkan wars of the 1990s. These factors have been and are barriers to the reception of Serbian music outside Serbia; its innovative qualities were often not appreciated as a result of its late introduction to foreign audiences. A lack of knowledge of the roots of Serbian music in folk and orthodox church music constitutes another factor impeding its appreciation. Milan Kundera reappears in this text with the formulation of the problem of 'universal music written in an unknown language' – a problem, however, which will not allow the composer to refrain from 'searching the melodic truth of the moment'.

The texts in this volume are based on presentations at a symposium organized by the University of Amsterdam in 2002. We believe, however, that their importance by far exceeds that occasion, and we are thankful for the opportunity of making the reflections of these authors available to a wider readership. We hope and expect that they will stimulate a more active and conscious attitude towards the reception of music, and a better understanding of the problems which new music must overcome before being accepted as part of our cultural capital. After all, each piece of music once upon a time was the newest music on earth.

Rokus de Groot
Albert van der Schoot

Part 1

Modernism and the development of style

In 1921 Arnold Schoenberg declares that because of him German music will continue to dominate the world for the next hundred years. Twelve years later he is forced to leave Germany forever. After the war, in America, laden with honours, he is still convinced that his work will be celebrated forever. He faults Igor Stravinsky for paying too much attention to his contemporaries and disregarding the judgment of the future. He expects posterity to be his most reliable ally. In a scathing letter to Thomas Mann he looks to the period 'after two or three hundred years,' when it will finally become clear which of the two was the greater, Mann or he! Schoenberg dies in 1951. For the next two decades his work is hailed as the greatest of the century, venerated by the most brilliant of the young composers, who declare themselves his disciples; but thereafter it recedes from both concert halls and memory. Who plays it nowadays, at the turn of this century? Who looks to him? No, I don't mean to make foolish fun of his presumptuousness and say he overestimated himself. A thousand times no! Schoenberg did not overestimate himself. He overestimated the future.

1 From: Milan Kundera, *Ignorance*, London 2002 Chapter 39, pp. 144-147.

Did he commit an error of thinking? No. His thinking was correct, but he was living in spheres that were too lofty. He was conversing with the greatest Germans, with Bach and Goethe and Brahms and Mahler, but, however intelligent they might be, conversations carried on in the higher stratospheres of the mind are always myopic about what goes on, with no reason or logic, down below: two great armies are battling to the death over sacred causes; but some minuscule plague bacterium comes along and lays them both low.

Schoenberg was aware that the bacterium existed. As early as 1930 he wrote: 'Radio is an enemy, a ruthless enemy marching irresistibly forward, and any resistance is hopeless'; it 'force-feeds us music ... regardless of whether we want to hear it, or whether we can grasp it,' with the result that music becomes just noise, a noise among other noises.

Radio was the tiny stream it all began with. Then came other technical means for reproducing, proliferating, amplifying sound, and the stream became an enormous river. If in the past people would listen to music out of love for music, nowadays it roars everywhere and all the time, 'regardless whether we want to hear it,' it roars from loudspeakers, in cars, in restaurants, in elevators, in the streets, in waiting rooms, in gyms, in the earpieces of Walkmans, music rewritten, reorchestrated, abridged, and stretched out, fragments of rock, of jazz, of opera, a flood of everything jumbled together so that we don't know who composed it (music become noise is anonymous), so that we can't tell beginning from end (music become noise has no form): sewage-water music in which music is dying.

Schoenberg saw the bacterium, he was aware of the danger, but deep inside he did not grant it much importance. As I said, he was living in the very lofty spheres of the mind, and pride kept him from taking seriously an enemy so small, so vulgar, so repugnant, so contemptible. The only great adversary worthy of him, the sublime rival whom he battled with verve and severity, was Igor Stravinsky. That was the music he charged at, sword flashing, to win the favor of the future.

But the future was a river, a flood of notes where composers' corpses drifted among the fallen leaves and torn-away branches. One day Schoenberg's dead body, bobbing about in the raging waves, collided with Stravinsky's, and in a shamefaced late-day reconciliation the two of them journeyed on together toward nothingness (toward the nothingness of music that is absolute din).[1]

Emotion has never been absent

EXILE OF MODERNISM
Klaas de Vries[2]

2 This text is based on
an interview with
Klaas de Vries conducted
by Rokus de Groot.

Kundera's novel *Ignorance* is about the experience of exile.
When the exile t-hinks about returning to the country he has
emigrated from, he expects to find it as he had left it. But in
fact, what he is to find does not even resemble the image of
the country as it was formed by his memory. When the exile
returns, he experiences complete alienation, because not only
the social and political situation has changed, but also what
was left of his personal connections. Kundera employs the
opposition between the attitudes of Stravinsky and Schoenberg
as an image of this, an opposition which was the subject of
Adorno's *Philosophie der Neuen Musik*, and which some
saw as representing the contrast between traditionalism and
modernism. Kundera describes this once vital opposition as
having become completely irrelevant to the musical and social
reality of today – the corpses of Schoenberg and Stravinsky
casually bump into each other among the flotsam and jetsam of
history.

Adorno in his time saw radio as the pervasive equalizer. He
described the experience of music as having no beginning or
end any more: we turn on the radio and we are engulfed by
music as a sound mass without shape. Listening with alert ears
no longer exists. This is the problem of non-listening.
This phenomenon of non-listening only increases. Even if we
try to find shelter against the numbing din, it is not possible,
because we have become so used to it. When recently I and
my son went to Antwerp, he took me to the shop he liked
best, in which we could not make ourselves heard, not even at
the counter, because of an unceasing loud drone. This drone
seemed completely undifferentiated. It was not determined by
musical factors, but by notions as 'this item is cool'. Why was
it cool? Because of the clip. Images are more important than
sound.

The question of traditionalism versus modernism has become
the object of a mock fight in our days. It has been overtaken
by history. We are exiles of a time when this issue was still

important. These times have gone, as has the exile's country from Kundera's *Ignorance*.

So if we still discuss issues of modernism and traditionalism, we engage with illusions. Instead we should be resisting advancing populism. We should be defending ourselves against the intended and unintentional attacks of commercialism. There are no more true modernists. As a resisting composer one should not enter into ideological debates, which tend to harden and become rigid, but concentrate on the essential values of European culture. For me it is not either Stravinsky or Schoenberg, but both Stravinsky and Schoenberg and much more, because of the values we share as the heirs to Western classical music: a concern with nuance, and a concern with authenticity. Whether music is good or bad is not at issue, what is at issue is that what one does must always be justifiable.

I detest the appeal to return to 'emotion'. Emotion has never been absent! It is very much present when I listen to Stockhausen's *Gruppen*. Listening to music which requires an intellectual effort, as for instance Guillaume de Machaut's music, yields an emotional experience. So why contrast cerebrality and emotionality?

What we should do is try to further the basic values of European culture. This does not equate with cultural tourism, which seems well developed at present. All foreigners visit the Van Gogh museum, they come to hear the Concertgebouworkest which is a very good orchestra. The concert hall is full, but one senses that the public's behaviour is completely ritualised. Performances are often perfect yet boring. There is no experience of the spirit of adventure as in the days when Eduard Flipse conducted the Rotterdam Phillharmonic Orchestra in the 1930s and '40s. He programmed every first performance, the latest Milhaud was played immediately in Rotterdam! Today's perfect but lifeless symphonic concerts are no antidote against commercial rubbish.

Is there nothing but lifeless perfection and commercialism? There is one positive side to our present situation. There is tolerance, however worn this notion may be. Tolerance in a simple sense, in that it bothers no one that rap-groups earn billions of dollars and are called geniuses while their music is of little artistic value, and in that it is acceptable that others view such groups as completely insignificant, while doing strange musical things which bring little financial gain. There is room for widely different behaviours and attitudes.
It is a matter of waves, the eternal coming and going of waves. At present the heirs to modern music are of only marginal importance. But from this margin we can start afresh. We might once again arrive at something like an 'inclusive concert' in Amsterdam's Carré. Or we might find ourselves in some underground premises in which something new is getting

underway. Not something already known, but something adventurous, something which reacts to our environment. I do not think that human beings ever change fundamentally. We never lose the need for sophistication. If I could not believe this, it would depress me indeed.

This does not mean that I reject commercialism as such. Commercial developments have made the technology for music composition easily accessible. Gone are the days in which we only had IRCAM, that symbol of arrogant inacessibility, housed underground, which required forms to be filled out in triplicate, and where we felt screened by Boulez in person. We were dependent on highly specialised sound engineers in laboratories. Today commercial production has enabled us to have our own 'laboratories' at home, which we can easily operate ourselves. This is my own experience. When composing A *King, riding* I started off in a very specialised IRCAM-like laboratory in Luik filled with huge machines, and finished work on an effective, simple, commercially developed sound system. Let us use the commercial systems with gratitude, and respond to them each in our own way.

The problem of non-listening remains however. Only a very few people are capable of listening; hardly anyone takes the trouble. I remember vividly the performance at a Holland Festival some years back of Berio's *Un re in ascolto*. It is a tragedy of listening. I have always experienced this work as if it were a requiem. A death ritual for European art. Berio's four hour burial of the ability to listen is a beautiful work, but it has something deeply melancholical about it.

The demise of listening can also be seen reflected in the Netherlands in the possible loss of classical music radio stations and radio orchestras, while the continuance of the adventurous concert series *Matinee op de vrije zaterdag* is under threat.

As a composer one has an obligation to further auditive receptivity, to open people's minds to new listening experiences and to musical discrimination. This is growing harder every day. Changes in educational policy have not only put listening to music under threat, but also listening in general. Children do not listen to a teacher; the nuances of the voice and of verbal exposition do not seem to matter. Pupils are given multiple choice questions, which seem unambiguous.

I remember quite well, while being a bad pupil at secondary school, that I only achieved good marks for Latin, even though I did not even like the language, much less than Greek anyway. But the Latin teacher's enthusiasm was absolutely contagious, in spite of the fact that he was quite modest and kept himself remote from the fashions of the day. He had charisma. His words were a revelation to me.

Today's generation of politicians tend to consider the modern music scene to be completely irrelevant. To them it is a music practice that has lost its self-evidence. They require justification. The problem is, it is hard to prove the relevance of the ability of auditive discrimination. He who has not even once been deeply touched by music, is deaf to arguments as to its relevance. To be touched by music is an unforgettable experience, one which I would not have missed for the world.

When I was fourteen years old I knew that I wanted to become a composer. The decisive occasion was a concert by the Groninger Orkestvereniging conducted by Van Epenhuizen in the music hall De Harmonie in Groningen. I was literally overwhelmed by the music. I was amazed. The music we listened to at home never exceeded Brahms. And now I had been presented with Bartók's *Concerto for orchestra*. The finale particularly came as somewhat of a shock. I had already been fascinated by this wonderful music right from the beginning, when to top it all the trumpet played. Later I discovered such moments in Bach's work as well, when one listens to music which is extraordinary in itself and then yet something extra is added! This is a really tremendous experience. At that time, as a fourteen-year old, I could not bear it. I was trembling with emotion. I had to leave the hall. Which was quite a feat, because the old building of the Harmonie had creaky floors. Once outside, I stood in front of the building for quite a while, stunned, bewildered. And I thought, although it was not quite a conscious thought: well, if a miracle like this happens to me, I must do something with it. The next day I went to the music bookshop, and I bought the score. As best I could I made a piano extract. This is how it all began for me. If a politician has never known such an experience, there is no point in discussing music policy with him. If he has never really listened, how then can he listen to arguments about new music?

A special feature of European music is notation. If there is no tradition of interpretation through listening to musicians who bring to life the values of nuance and authenticity, one can read scores without understanding. Only very few interpreters can cause sublime experiences to happen. Sviatoslav Richter is one of them. He remains true to the score in a meticulous yet completely personal way. I am very enthusiastic about his attention to minute details. He makes me feel that this is what music is all about. Actually, what he does is quite mysterious.

I try to compose works about which I think that I am the only one who could have written them. This sounds arrogant, but I think that it is the only way one can justify one's work. I try to write music which I would like to hear very much, and the like of which I have not heard in any other composer's works. This is what authenticity means to me. To me the modernist period is part of the tradition of authenticity. I have no inclination to repeat *Gruppen*, or to recompose Mahler's music. Of course *Gruppen* can be relevant to me at a certain time, or Mahler or Machaut. But a composer should relate to music history in an authentic way and avoid being some sort of cultural tourist.

I am not a composer who constructs his works from theory. When I write a rigourous work, as for instance *Versus* for the Nederlands Blazersensemble, with many forms of mirroring, I immediately tend to undermine this rigour. Sometimes I feel frustrated that from such a composition as *Versus* I am unable to distill something that I could call my own language. I go in search of my music time and again, with every new composition. At the same time this very much belongs to the European tradition, the urge to transgress the boundaries of our musical thought.

However, if we no longer share a common understanding of music, it becomes very difficult to justify the endeavour of reaching for great depths of listening with relatively few people. Such an endeavour must find a more general acceptance. Unfortunately, radio policy seems to be a competition in popularisation, dictated by the need to attract listeners and increase ratings.

What has happened to modernism? Is it to go down into history as a failed experiment, as no more than the corpses of Schoenberg and Stravinsky in Kundera's novel? Or is it part of a larger European tradition based on the values of nuance and authenticity, which is still vital, temporarily marginalised, yet ready to flourish again?

Some dissonances
are more equal
than others

BACK TO THE FUTURE
Albert van der Schoot

1 Milan Kundera,
Ignorance, London
2002, p. 143.

> For how can a person with no knowledge of the future
> understand the meaning of the present? [1]

Music history is not a natural phenomenon: it is man-made.
This may seem a truism, yet it is an aspect of music life which
generally escapes the attention of the average concert-goer.
What makes the listener listen to one piece of music rather
than to another? The intended public is faced with a pre-
printed concert hall programme from which to make a choice.
Compositions and composers are listed in an orderly way, and
the listeners know more or less what to expect from whom.
If they are interested, music history books will refresh their
memories as to which composers and which styles belong
where in music history. But all this is presented as the heritage
of the past. There are few incentives to make listeners realise
they are listening to something which, once upon a time, was
not yet there; listeners find themselves confronted with a
completed *forma formata* rather than with a developing *forma
formans*.

Do composers merely sway to the rhythm of the spirit
of their age, providing history with the suitable musical
accompaniment that happens to belong to that age? Or can
they, by conscious reflection upon the present state and
possible further developments, make a difference to the future
course of music?
I would like to go back in time to a few moments in history
in which composers presented their views about music that
had not yet come into existence – the music of the future of
the past. It is important to become aware of their ideas not
as historical data, as history already made, but as part of the
process of history in the making.

I strongly believe that the best way of handling the present
and designing the future is by understanding the past, but also
that the best way of understanding the past is by imagining it
as a once-upon-a-time future – that is, as a situation in which
choices had to be made, which had to be accounted for.
Why should the history of music be a history of styles anyway?
If a style satisfies musicians and audience, why not stick to it,

rather than go through the cumbersome process of inventing something new?

Schoenberg wrote, in one of his articles on *New Music*: 'The real causes of changes in the style of musical compositions are others'.[2] Schoenberg meant that (other) artists are bound to react to the world which they encounter. He emphasises that if a certain style has been *in vogue* for some time, young composers have no choice but to rebel against it, for the very reason that anything new wears down and needs replacing. There is no point in creating something if it is not new. Schoenberg: '(....) if a man is anxious to be widely listened to, it is up to him to say something the others *did not know before*, but would be better off for knowing'.[3]

Each piece of music is new music before it eventually belongs to that pre-printed concert hall programme through which *forma formans* solidifies into music history. Music history is, indeed, man-made; but this implies that, at any specific moment in time, it is history in the making. It is only afterwards that we begin to feel comfortable with the terminology of such and such a style; significant concepts for style characteristics come about only with hindsight, in their description by analysts and historians. It is their efforts which make a style intelligible, and therefore theoretically accessible and communicable. Would Palestrina have been able to explain to us the rules of Palestrinian counterpoint?

He would probably not have been at a complete loss for words, had he been asked; but the full syntax of his style was spelled out only in 1725, by Johann Joseph Fux.

Palestrina never knew the rules of his own counterpoint, the most fully defined style in music history, as intimately as generations of composers who were educated in times when Palestrinian counterpoint had long gone out of fashion. Yet it became the gateway that provided access to the development of the styles of these newer generations. On the other hand, new music also helps us to listen to old-fashioned counterpoint with our ears wide open. We hear it, so to say, from another angle, or in another perspective. This is the process which hermeneuticians refer to as *Wirkungsgeschichte*, and it works for music in basically the same way as for texts (which hermeneuticians prefer to refer to): our understanding today is informed by the past, and at the same time, that very past is understood today from our present perspective. The consequence of this mutual relationship is that the past never remains the same.

History did not only decide *which* music we listen to, but also *how* we listen to it. There are styles of listening, just as there are styles of composing. The reception of earlier music is dependent on the listening style which we now have at our command, to a far greater degree than the composer's contemporaries would have had; but the fact that we have

2 Arnold Schoenberg, *Style and Idea*, London 1975, p. 115.

3 *Style and Idea*, p. 100.

learned to master this style is due to the very music from the past that we have been listening to.

Conquering time

To my knowledge, the first conscious attempt to not only create or interpret another new *piece* of music, but to pave the way for a new *style* of musical composition, dates from the beginning of the 14th century. Philippe de Vitry and Johannes de Muris are to be credited for theoretically underpinning the breakaway from the musical style which, with hindsight, found a place in music history under the name of *Ars antiqua*. The very titles *Ars nova* and *Ars novae musicae*, under which their respective treatises have become known, suggest that these theoreticians were indeed conscious of the innovative character of the changes they were proclaiming.[4]
Should this be considered a case in which theoretical reflections did effectively lead to a change in musical style? I believe that, to a certain degree, this is indeed the case. Compare the French motet as it flourished in the second half of the 13th century with the motet style as it developed in the beginning of the 14th century: the motets from the *Roman de Fauvel* and, later, those by Guillaume de Machaut. The former motets stem from a world which is, one might say, all-embracing; the texts of their separate parts may simultaneously reflect very different spheres of life, be they religious or secular, expressed in Latin or in French, and unite them synchronously in much the same way in which Aquinas's *Summa* unites the spheres of knowledge, reason and belief into one encompassing ontology. Such motets bear testimony to the 'great chain of being', reflected in the spiritual sphere by the one unified Church, as yet unchallenged by any call for reformation.
Both Philippe de Vitry and Johannes de Muris engage in an investigation which will lead to a focal shift within this encompassing ontology – an investigation into the relationship between 'time' and 'event'. *Sound*, being an event generated by motion, 'belongs to the class of successive things', as Johannes de Muris wrote[5] (music is a *transitory* art, as we would now say), whereas *time* 'belongs to the class of continuous things'.[6] The old opposition between an ontology of being and an ontology of becoming determines the primacy between the two: 'Time inseparably unites motion. Therefore it follows necessarily that time is the measure of sound.'[7]
The *Ars nova*-'programme' from the early 14th century betrays an awareness of time as the organizing factor of movement, which had not yet come into being in earlier periods. This enabled musicians to standardize the notation of their volatile art; specifically: to codify the relationship between binary and ternary divisions, and to replace the initially less

4 This suggestion, though, may be too strong. *Ars nova* is now considered to be an anonymous treatise based on Philippe de Vitry's teachings, whereas the correct title of the 1321 treatise by Johannes de Muris reads *Notitia artis musicae*. In this article, I will stick to the texts and titles as given by Strunk.

5 Johannes de Muris, *Ars novae musicae*, in *Source readings in music history* (ed. O. Strunk), New York/London 1965, Vol. I, p. 172.

6 *Ars novae musicae*, p. 174.

7 *Ars novae musicae*, p. 172.

Modernism and the development of style

systematically applied *ligatures* and other temporary solutions for temporal problems with a well-ordered mensural system. In order to discover whether such a reform does indeed entail a major shift in music history, we must ask ourselves the question: *was there any opposition against it?* If not, we may assume that such a new theory merely phrases changes that were experienced generally, and whose documentation met with approval from the musical establishment. But if there was opposition, this may indicate that someone felt threatened, and that we are faced with a musical paradigm shift in which a 'new style' distances itself from an old style.

A reliable indication that Philippe de Vitry and Johannes de Muris were really breaking new ground is the fact that their treatises aroused the fury of the more conservative theoreticians of their age. In his *Speculum musicae*, Jacob of Liège grumbles at his younger colleagues for their 'corrupting what is perfect with many imperfections'[8] – not for speculative ends, which would be more or less acceptable, but by putting these imperfections into practice. This is a serious threat to existing order – not only to musical order, but also to the social/religious certainties of the *Ars antiqua* period; '(f)or he who deserts truth deserts God, since God is truth'.[9]

Jacob fears the new conceptions of time which the *Ars nova* theorists proclaim: 'Now in our day have come new and more recent authors, writing on mensurable music, little revering their ancestors, the ancient doctors; nay, rather changing their sound doctrine in many respects, corrupting, reproving, annulling it, they protest against it in word and deed when the civil and mannerly thing to do would be to defend and expound them. Considering these things in the modern manner of singing and still more in the modern writings, I was grieved.'[10]

This is not the kind of expression of opinion we find in earlier texts, e.g. in Aristoxenus' *Harmonics*, on whether musical tones should be judged by reason or by the ear; or in Plato's *Republic*, where Socrates tries to determine the tone scales to be recommended for education purposes. This is a moment of choice which results from a historical development, a choice between two alternative attitudes; and although the terminology of the treatises often seems overly technical and not very inviting to non-musicians, the controversy exceeds the bounds of mere musical preference. The modernists of the early 14th century were instrumental in opening up a different world view, in which cohesion is not granted by the great chain of being as it was instituted by God's Creation, but by the homogeneity within that Creation. We may compare their new awareness of time with the new awareness of space as it was expressed by authors like Alberti in the 15th century. A vague consciousness of space as a condition for extensiveness became more acute and accurate as painters discovered and developed

8 Jacob of Liège, *Speculum musicae*, book VII, in *Source readings*, Vol. I, p. 183.

9 *Speculum musicae*, p.182.

10 *Speculum musicae*, p.181.

the laws of perspective; and again: an implicit background notion became explicit as an organizing factor. Needless to say that this caused a revolutionary change in the whole art of visual representation.

One could argue that mensural notation, as it was elaborated by the *Ars nova*-theoreticians, is the material condition for a perspective-theory of time: it allows the composer to imagine time-as-structure, *before* this time is filled with actual sound – just as the Renaissance painters acquired the ability to imagine the structure of space as independent from the objects filling that space. Even if several of the *Ars nova* innovations were already anticipated by composers in the second half of the 13th century, notably Franco of Cologne and Pierre de la Croix, the teachings and writings of Philippe de Vitry and Johannes de Muris were decisive in the further permeation of a new spirit and its effects on musical practice.

The Camerata

An even more striking example of musical innovation prompted by theoretical speculation is to be found in the appearance of the Florentine *Camerata*. This movement provides us with a surprising attempt towards musical innovation *by rejecting the new rather than the old*.

The Florentine intelligentsia that gathered at the home of count Giovantni de' Bardi, during the last decades of the 16th century, had developed a strong antipathy towards the polyphonic style as it had developed in Italy since the arrival of Northern European composers – 'the Goths', as they were disdainfully referred to by the Camerata adherents.

The scope of their orientation was – not surprisingly for a group of Renaissance humanists – the idealised and idolized culture of Antiquity. Yet in this respect the 'musicologists' of the Renaissance were in a very different position from the men of letters – for what had ancient music theory and practice been like? The influential theorist Vincenzo Galilei tried to restore the practice of ancient Greek music and theory from scanty data inherited from antiquity. The result was that some scattered remarks concerning the place and function of music in society, and the relative importance of text and melody, were inflated to testimonies to a complete and coherent theory of music, on which a reformation of musical style could be based. To the humanist educator Galilei, it seemed to be beyond doubt that polyphony was due to a regrettable misunderstanding, and that the modern composers, should they be informed of the true aim and nature of music, would immediately see and correct the error of their ways.

In his *Dialogo della musica antica e della moderna* (1581), he has Count Bardi (who in the *Dialogue* acts as a spokesman for the Camerata) explain:

> (....) if the practice of music, I say, was introduced among men for the reason and object that all the learned concur in declaring, namely, if it arose primarily to express the passions with greater effectiveness in celebrating the praises of the gods, the genii, and the heroes, and secondarily to communicate these with equal force to the minds of mortals for their benefit and advantage, then it will be clear that the rules observed by the modern contrapuntists as inviolable laws, as well as those they often use from choice and to show their learning, will be directly opposed to the perfection of the true and best harmonies and melodies. It will not be difficult to prove and demonstrate this to them convincingly, for when they recall all that has thus far been said on this subject, they will set aside their own interest and their envy, wrong practice, and ignorance.[11]

In order to understand the need for a new style of composition, we must understand the reasons for rejecting the old. The major stumbling-block was the fact that the polyphonic style of composing, with its independent voice leading texture, made it impossible for the music to follow the ideas and the moods expressed in the text, and for the listener to understand the text in the first place. As a result, the melodic line lost its self-evident function of supporting the text, even in melodies which were not part of a polyphonic texture. This objection was shared by the church: Pope Gregory XIII's letter to Palestrina and Zoilo, requesting them to revise the choir books used in the church, has survived as a significant document in music history. In this letter, the pope called upon the two composers to purify the choir books from the 'barbarisms and obscurities' that had been added, under the influence of the new style in composition, even to the unisonous Gregorian melodies. To the ears of the *Curia*, this prevented the Graduals and other choir books of the time from 'reverently, distinctly, and devoutly' praising God's name.[12] Gregory's request, dated October 25, 1577, was a late result of the discussions at the Council of Trent (1545-1563); the outstretched time-frame indicates that the need for reform was experienced as an important issue during a major part of the late 16th century. And if this need was felt even for Gregorian plainchant, how much stronger must papal ears have been offended by the four-, eight- or even sixteen-part motets and masses that were also composed in these decades!

Ecclesiastical and secular objections to polyphony thus went hand in hand. Yet secular objections were to have the greater impact on the further course of music history. Palestrina never finished his assignment (others did, in 1614), but the Camerata circle in an unprecedented way managed to change

Back to the future

11 Vincenzo Galilei, *Dialogo della musica antica e della moderna*, in *Source readings*, Vol. II, pp. 116/7.

12 *Brief on the Reform of the Chant*, in *Source readings*, Vol. II, pp. 168/9.

musical practice on the basis of theoretical speculation; the monodic style became what Monteverdi would call a *seconda prattica* next to the 'modern', but now old-fashioned *prima prattica* of polyphony. Galilei and the other Camerata scholars succeeded as innovators precisely because they failed as the restorers they intended to be. How favourable their innovation was, and how quickly it became successful, can be concluded from the fast dissemination of monody over Italy and over the rest of Europe. It can also be illustrated by the preface of Giulio Caccini's collection of madrigals *Le nuove musiche*, published in Florence in 1602. Caccini, who worked under the personal influence of Count Bardi and was one of the very first composers to implement the Camerata ideals in the new style of *dramma per musica*, proudly reminds his readers that he was personally present with the intellectual *fine fleur* of Florence at the Camerata sessions in Bardi's home. He leaves no doubt about the question whether the theoretical discussions had any impact on his compositorial practice:

13 Giulio Caccini,
Le nuove musiche
(1602), ed. W.Hitchcock,
Madison 1982, p. 44.

> I can truly say that I gained more from their learned discussions than from my more than thirty years of counterpoint. For these most knowledgeable gentlemen kept encouraging me, and with the most lucid reasoning convinced me, not to esteem that sort of music which, preventing any clear understanding of the words, shatters both their form and content, now lengthening and now shortening syllables to accommodate the counterpoint (a laceration of the poetry!) but rather to conform to that manner so lauded by Plato and other philosophers (who declared that music is naught but speech, with rhythm and tone coming after; not vice versa) with the aim that it enter into the minds of men and have those wonderful effects admired by the great writers. But this has not been possible because of the counterpoint of modern music (....).[13]

Caccini's enthusiasm should not make us forget to ask our test question: *was there any opposition against the new style*? There was. The main target was Monteverdi, who turned out to be the most talented among the young composers who felt attracted to the Camerata ideas. The role of Jacob of Liège was now played by Giovanni Maria Artusi. In the year in which Caccini and Peri staged their first opera, this cleric from Bologna published his *Delle imperfezioni della moderna musica*, also known as *L'Artusi*.

The very title shows that the new style, which had been intended as an old style, had struck root: the modern music which Artusi attacks is the music of the madrigalists of the day – music which freely makes use of uncommon harmonies and dissonances to better express the emotions suggested by the text. The old style which Artusi defends is the very 'musica moderna' that had been the target of Galilei's *Dialogue* – the music governed by the rules of counterpoint. Artusi has the following piece of hard-boiled logic in store to undermine the harmonic experiments of those composers who insist on breaking traditional rules:

> Now, even if you wish dissonance to become consonant, it remains necessary that it be contrary to consonance; by nature it is always dissonant and can hence become consonant only when consonance becomes dissonant; this brings us to impossibilities, although these new composers may perhaps so exert themselves that in the course of time they will discover a new method by which dissonance will become consonance, and consonance dissonance.[14]

In the same period in which the first operas were successfully staged in the cities of Italy, an English scholar was brooding on the best way to plan and reform society. Like Vincenzo Galilei in Italy, Francis Bacon looked back to an imaginary past in order to achieve a better future; and like his contemporary Galileo Galilei, he set out to challenge the authority of Aristotelian convictions of nature by confronting traditionally accepted knowledge with the results of his own experiments. The 'Great Instauration' which he had in mind aimed at a 'general Renewal of the sciences and arts and of all human learning'.[15]

Although Bacon was not directly involved with music and lacked the competence to consider the future of musical styles, I still do not want to pass him by here, because of the few words he devotes to music in his *New Atlantis*. The European shipwrecked sailors coming ashore on the island of Bensalem, far away in the Pacific Ocean, are amazed to find a research institute there dedicated to the improvement of human living conditions. Acoustic living conditions are no exception to this; in perfect Spanish, the father of *Solomon's House* (the scientific institution) explains to the Europeans:

> We have also sound-houses, where we practise and demonstrate all sounds, and their generation. We have harmonies which you have not, of quarter-sounds, and lesser slides of sounds.
> Divers instruments of music likewise to you unknown, some sweeter than any you have; together with bells and rings that are dainty and sweet. We represent small sounds as great and deep; likewise great sounds extenuate and sharp; we make divers tremblings and warblings of sounds, which in their original are entire.
> We represent and imitate all articulate sounds and letters, and the voices and notes of beasts and birds. We have certain helps which set to the ear do further the hearing greatly.
> We have also divers strange and artificial echoes, reflecting the voice many times, and as it were tossing it: and some that give back the voice louder than it came; some shriller, and some deeper; yea, some rendering the voice differing in the letters

14 Giovanni M. Artusi, *Delle imperfezioni della moderna musica*, in *Source readings*, Vol. III, p. 40.

15 Francis Bacon, *The New Organon* (1620), eds. L. Jardine & M. Silverthorne, Cambridge 2000, p. 2.

or articulate sound from that they receive. We have also means
to convey sounds in trunks and pipes, in strange lines and
distances.[16]

European readers of the 21st century must surely be amazed
to find this utopian vision in a text from the early 17th century
rather than in the user's manual of some recently developed
electronic device. Practically each and every element of
this description is familiar to us, as the results of technical
developments that we associate exclusively with the 20th
century. Any synthesizer can illustrate each of the effects
described here. So this is how Francis Bacon imagined the
possibilities of the future.
Nevertheless, in all its sagacity, this is a vision on the
development of *sound technology*, not of music history.

Although there have been enough quarrels about music in
the centuries that followed, often focussing on the ancient
issue of the primacy of text over melody, it is worth noting
that stylistic change in these centuries, the music of which
eventually became known as the 'iron repertory', came about
without any advanced planning. It is not until Wagner that
we find a major composer planning the 'Artwork of the
Future'. Bach and Handel, Haydn, Mozart and Beethoven,
Schubert and Brahms did not indulge in *designing* a musical
future in theory any more than did Palestrina – they simply
created their future. Important books of theory by others that
were published during their lifetimes (like those by Rameau,
Mattheson, Fétis) did not aim at creating a new style, but
at underpinning the structure of music as it had already
developed. The whole process of the emancipation of music
towards the sovereign status of an 'absolute art', even the most
absolute of all arts, resulted from an inner development in
musical practice, not from a theoretically founded resistance
against an existing practice. This new status found its
metaphysical glorification in Schopenhauer's *Die Welt als Wille
und Vorstellung* (1819) and its aesthetic defence in Hanslick's
Vom musikalisch Schönen (1854), but neither Schopenhauer
nor Hanslick would claim any fame for bringing that status
about. They describe music as (they believe) it *is*, not as it
should come into being. No ideology has guided music in
this process of liberation from the reins of drama and text
– a process which I believe to be one of the most exciting
achievements in the cultural history of mankind.

The flight into the future

Another three hundred years after Monteverdi, Artusi and
Bacon, Arnold Schoenberg did not waste time rebelling
against the past – he simply outgrew it. What was impossible

16 *New Atlantis* (1626),
in *The Works of
Francis Bacon*, Vol. III,
eds. J. Spedding a.o.,
London 1887,
pp. 162/3.

to imagine for Artusi in early Baroque Bologna became reality in the capital of the dissolving Habsburg empire. The polarity between consonance and dissonance dissolved as well, and with it some of the other polarities that were connected with tonality: tonic vs. dominant or subdominant, and ultimately melody vs. harmony. 18th century discussions concerning the primacy of melody or harmony (such as the confrontations in France, involving Rameau, Rousseau and many others) had become pointless. It is important to realise that the habit of thinking in terms of polarities was not dictated by any *musical* laws; rather, it was the way of thinking characteristic for the whole of the 19th century, in Germany even more so than elsewhere, and it had been codified around 1800 by several philosophers, scientists and other authors – the first being Schelling and Goethe. (It was Goethe himself who tried to transplant his style of thinking in polarities to the field of music, when he started out to design a *Tonlehre* after the model of his *Farbenlehre*, with the polarity between major and minor modes replacing the *Urpolarität* between light and dark. He never got beyond the first few pages.)

What was left when, in the declining years of romanticism, polarity lost its ground? In his 1911 *Harmonielehre*, Schoenberg considered the emancipation of the dissonance to be an inevitable result of the evolution of harmonic means.[17] The distinction between consonances and dissonances is only gradual: dissonances are 'hidden' within the overtone row of each tone just as well as consonances are, so it had to be merely a matter of time before they would come to the fore. The synchrony of Schoenberg's analysis with the analytical practice of his fellow-townsman Sigmund Freud is unmistakable: 'The more remote overtones are recorded by the subconscious, and when they ascend into the conscious they are analyzed and their relation to the total sound is determined.'[18] Music seems to undergo psycho-analytical treatment, in order to come to grips with the traumas from its childhood, traumas such as the threatening *Querstände* and the generally feared *diabolus in musica*. Once such inhibitions have passed the threshold of musical consciousness, they will no longer be experienced as a threat for harmony. And this forms the basis for Schoenberg's prediction that the terminological polarity between consonance and dissonance will soon be outmoded. About ten years later, Schoenberg was to present his own 'method' of 'composition with twelve tones related only to one another'. And with hindsight, the MGG (*Musik in Geschichte und Gegenwart*) does indeed credit Schoenberg with having 'solved the crisis of tonality'.

There are several reasons why it is more difficult in this than in the two other cases to answer the question whether theoretical reflection preceded and directed a change in compositorial practice. A first reason is that, with Schoenberg,

17 Arnold Schoenberg, *Harmonielehre*, Vienna 1911; English edition: *Theory of Harmony*, London 1978.

18 *Theory of Harmony*, pp. 20/1.

the bulk of his writings on 'new music' did not so much precede his new style, but rather developed over the same period (the already mentioned *Harmonielehre* is not a blueprint of the later dodecaphonic practice). A second reason is the lack of fit between what Schoenberg actually does with the tones and his own description of that practice. The twelve tones cease to be related to functional tonality; but does that imply that they are 'related only to one another', as Schoenberg says? It is this very *relationship* to one another which the listener desperately tries to establish. Was not tonality, in one form or another, the very basis of that relationship between the tones? If you really have no idea which tone to expect next, you can hardly be surprised if it turns out to be a different one. Non-existing expectations can neither be confirmed nor thwarted.

And finally, a third reason: in the 20th century, the relationship between music theory and music practice itself has changed. I believe the answer to the question whether Schoenberg's theory preceded an innovation in composing must ultimately be affirmative, but in a more sophisticated way than in earlier periods of music history. It is impossible for a composer in the 20th century to use his (or anybody else's) musical language intuitively, as a native speaker; he will also be held responsible for having chosen *this* particular idiom, and not another, as his means of expression (if expression is still on the menu).

As for our survey into the contemporary reception of the new development: in the case of Schoenberg, an affirmative answer to the question *was there any opposition against the new style?* can hardly be anything but an understatement. The question *was there anything but opposition?* seems to be more appropriate. The Jacobs of Liège and the Artusis of Schoenberg's time were easily outnumbered by the ranks of newspaper critics and audiences that attended his concerts and could not wait to express their disapproval.

This was the reaction that led Schoenberg to the conviction that he had to flee from the present and seek shelter in the future. This attitude seems to give strength to the idea that composers make their individual choices, including the choice to meet their doom; but this is misleading. What composers do is *engage themselves in a project*; such an engagement may be considered a choice, but it is not an arbitrary choice that might just as well have turned out differently. As Schoenberg's own attitude shows, he felt compelled to do what he did. He tended to consider his career as the completion of his fate rather than as an individual choice, in the belief that what he did had to be done anyway, so why not by him?

There is an undeniable similarity between the way the Camerata scholars outgrew Renaissance counterpoint, and the way Schoenberg and his followers left the Wagnerian abundance of harmony behind. In both cases a consciously planned innovation in music history is breaking new ground, but it finds its aesthetic ideal in a reduction rather than in an expansion of its means. The message is one of reformation rather than of revolution; the future is disguised in a 'back to...'-story, as the removal of barriers that have been put up to impede the free development of musical possibilities. We find this same tendency among Schoenberg's contemporaries, who innovated compositorial practice with different means. Bartók, e.g., moves away from the diatonic scale in two directions simultaneously: he expands it towards chromaticism (yet without any suggestion that the twelve tones should be considered equal), and he reduces it to pentatony. This leads to a completely new and crystal clear musical language, in which pentatony leads chromaticism, not the other way round. Bartók's writings leave no doubt (nor do his compositions) as to where his own sympathies lie: the monophony of pentatonic folk song is to be the foundation for the further development of any type of more complicated music, be it homophonic, heterophonic or polyphonic. This new musical language is designed explicitly in order to bridge the gap between the social occasions in which folk music is a living practice and the concert hall which is to ensure that art music will continue to have a future at all, whichever this may be. If we ask the question: *did these extra-musical considerations lead to a lasting effect in (a) musical style*? I think the answer must again be positive, with the *caveat* that this effect was geographically much more restricted than in the case of Schoenberg. Among present-day composers, György Kurtág presents the best example of a style descending directly from Bartók. And even more than with Bartók himself, Kurtág's minimalist compositions are based on an utter reduction of the musical material, a *Microcosmos* to the square. Yet it remains musical material, not blind atomism.

Such a follow-up is different from Schoenberg's. The Vienna School abolished traditional melody as well as functional harmony, and was thus left with other parameters whose job became inevitably more important in creating the musical tension necessary to keep the listener's interest alive. Schoenberg and his direct followers proved that this can be done: utter concentration on rhythm, tone colour, dynamics and form makes it possible to renounce traditional melody and harmony, and still reach a certain degree of expression. This calls for a benevolent audience willing to engage in a project that deprives the listener of the most accessible means of expression, which continue to be linked with tonality. The experience of the past decades has taught us that, as Schoenberg's adherents had hoped when they founded the *Verein für musikalische Privataufführungen*, such an audience can indeed be brought into existence. But by presenting his way of composing as a 'method', Schoenberg also paved the way for those who were indeed able to apply that method to sound combinations, but were not able to compose music. Many of those who followed the post-war courses on *neue Musik* in Darmstadt belong in that category.

All tones, all intervals, all chords and other harmonic phenomena may officially be declared equal, yet they will turn out not to be so. Or, to vary Orwell's well-known dictum: some dissonances are more equal than others. Music can do without the mixolydian scale, the subdominant, the *basso continuo*, the sonata form or complementary rhythm, but not without one basic condition: *tension and release*. In so far as a piece of music should not just be the outcome of a calculation, but an acoustic phenomenon to be *listened* to, to receive aural attention, the listener needs the possibility to identify with a process, in which in one way or another the next note sounds *as if it belongs*, which implies that it should relate to the previous note. Quite independent of any music theoretical interpretation, this seems to be a psychological prerequisite. Needless to say that the capacities of listeners in this respect diverge widely; and also that, as the case of Schoenberg shows, such capacities can (fortunately) be developed further. But if the reason for the next note to be there is merely the fact that it is, say, the last one of the dodecaphonic series being wound off, then it is reduced to being nothing but the outcome of a calculation. Over 99% of listeners will not be able to follow that logic acoustically, so if that were the only reason for that note to be there, such music remains inaccessible to the audience. It takes compositorial skill, insight in building up and reducing musical tension, to make such a note worthwhile listening to, whether or not it has a certain position in a series. This is why Schoenberg, Berg and Webern have eventually become part of the living tradition of music history, and Darmstadt was left to that part of music theory which never struck root in music practice.

The rhythm is pumped in from outside

RHYTHM AND LIFE IN MUSIC
Roger Scruton

Each movement of a Bach or Handel suite is described with the name of a dance: allemande, gigue, sarabande, minuet and so on. Overtures, fugues, preludes, passacaglias and sonatas are not named after dances; nevertheless, dance rhythms can often be heard in them, and even the most intellectually demanding of Bach's instrumental works are characterised by strong rhythmic profiles which may set the feet tapping and the body swaying in sympathy. In this chapter I want to draw attention to the uses of rhythm in classical and modern music, and to point to various misconceptions about the nature of rhythm and dancing that have crept into current thinking on the topic.

There is a distinction to be made between dance-rhythm and song-rhythm, the first supporting physical movement, the second supporting melody. These may overlap, but they originate in distinct musical uses. Thus a dance rhythm must be regular if it is to move ordinary people to dance; it must set up a beat and an accent, into which steps and formations can be fitted. Whether it also has a melodic line is comparatively unimportant, although a tune of sorts will help people to move along with the music. Contrast folk dancing (e.g. Scottish Ceilidh), with lyrical folk-song – the latter often wandering far from the beat, and taking its rhythmic organisation from the melodic line itself, as in 'Oh! Waly, Waly'.

Of course, most folk traditions mix song and dance, and many of the dance-forms which entered the classical idiom were also song-forms – the Chaconne, for example. Much classical Arab music shows rhythm generated within, and as it were extended from, a melodic line, with the percussion following the melody and often dividing beats in response to divisions in the note values of the melody. Although you can sometimes dance to the beat of this music, its primary purpose is to give a metrical frame to the song. Such music has a ritornello structure, but without regular periods designed for dancing.

Dance rhythms in Bach and Handel are a matter of measure, accent and beat within the melody. Accompanying figures are rare, and do not have the rhythmic function that they were to acquire in later classical music. Thanks in part to the Ländler and Waltz – folk dances which entered classical music by way of self-conscious tribute to popular culture – composers began to generate rhythm through accompanying figures, which became the main vehicle of metrical energy in the music. A consummate example of this is the trio from the scherzo of Dvorák's New World symphony. Contrast this with the last movement of Beethoven's seventh symphony – the movement that Wagner described as 'the apotheosis of the dance' – in which the stupendous rhythmic energy is generated entirely within the melodic line. This is of course not so much a dance as a symphonic reflection on the dance.

Even in the Dvorák, however, the accompanying figure has a melodic organisation, and the rhythm is generated internally, without recourse to percussion or obtrusive downbeats. This imparts to the music its striking lilt, and also creates a desire to move with it – for it is already moving, pointing the way, as it were, as when one person leads another on to the dance-floor. This is very different from the ostinato, in which the music is measured out by a persistent beat quite independently of the melodic organisation. Stravinsky in *Oedipus Rex* sustains the chorus with an ostinato 6/8 beat, on G and B flat, and the result is rhythmical but static. You have no desire to dance to or with this music, even if it carries you along compulsively. The rhythm is like an external force, constraining the music from outside.

The extreme case of this phenomenon, in which rhythm is detached from harmonic and melodic organisation, and fired at them from another and extra-musical place, is the rhythmic 'backing' of synthetic pop. This might have a mechanical 'tic-toc' character, as in 'No Son of Mine' by the group Genesis (from the appropriately named album, *We Can't Dance*); or it may depend upon mixing, in which melody and harmony are smeared into a soup, leaving only percussive ostinato to establish some kind of measure – as in 'Be Here Now' by the group Oasis. Here rhythm has fallen away from the music altogether, leaving a bare shell of melody and a harmonic progression without cogent voice leading, both overwhelmed by the percussive noise from next door.

You might say of such music that it has beat, but not rhythm. Rhythm is the inner life of music. Beat without rhythm is a rigid frame on which the music is pinned and crucified. It is possible to recognize in the idiom adopted by Oasis a disaggregation of music into beat and pitch, neither giving true support to the other. The drum-kit has the role of marshalling the music to its stride, forbidding all deviation, while adding nothing to the melodic or harmonic development. (Contrast the Dvořák; here the lilting phrase that generates the rhythm is also replete with melodic and harmonic implications, which subsequently unfold through the melodic line.)

The use made by the drum-kit in contemporary pop is to a great extent an innovation. Classical jazz introduced the drum-kit as a way of embellishing a pre-existing rhythm, often sounded on the offbeat and hidden, as it were, behind the strumming of the banjo. The rhythm was generated by the syncopated voices of the instruments, each of which played its part in breathing rhythmic life into the bar-lines. The result is not so very far from a Courante or Gigue by Bach. Strictly speaking, New Orleans jazz has no need of percussion, which it uses – if at all – purely ornamentally. In modern pop percussion has a constitutive, rather than an ornamental use: without it, there would be no music, since the beat – on which everything depends – would not exist.

In the early days of rock you find a jazz-like use of the drum-kit – not to impose a rhythm synthesized outside the melodic line, but to emphasize and vary a rhythm generated within it. The *locus classicus* of this is Elvis Presley, whose extraordinary voice, with its barely perceptible micro-rhythms and tremors, produces melody and rhythm together, so that the one is inseparable from the other. In 'Heartbreak Hotel', for example, the rhythm is compelling announced by the solo voice, and the bass seems merely to take it up and prolong it.

Equally impressive in this respect is Eric Clapton, who uses the guitar rather as Elvis uses his voice, to set the music in motion before the drum-kit enters, so establishing the rhythmical identity of the piece as an internal feature. ('Lay Down Sally' is an effective instance.)

The new attitude to rhythm is connected with a new attitude to dancing. The dance-forms adopted by Bach and Handel were attached to elaborate rituals and courtesies, and required complicated steps and formations from the dancers. They were group dances, in which partners were often exchanged, and in which people of all ages could participate without embarrassment. In a very real sense the dancers were themselves generating the rhythm that controlled them, and generating it together, by attentive gestures in which courtesy was an important element. The experience of dancing as a 'dancing with' (usually with a partner as part of a group, subsequently, as a result of the waltz, with a single partner) survived right down to the days of rock and roll and the twist. Then, almost overnight, it disappeared.

Dancing today does not involve complicated steps or formations; it does not even involve contact with the partner, or indeed any partner at all. Moreover it is not really open to people of all ages, but confined to the young and the sexually available. The pulse sets the dance in motion and controls its beat, but it does nothing to suggest how or with whom you should move. There is a puppet-like quality to the dancer, and the dance, like the rhythm, remains external to the music. You see this at its most extreme in techno-rock, especially when embellished with strobe lights and psychedelic effects. Such dancing is like throwing oneself into a pool of collective emotion, to be swept away in its frenzy. There is nothing you can do, either to create or to embellish the rhythm. And communication with a partner is rendered impossible by the noise, the lights and the sheer formless press of the crowd to every side. Sarabandes and galliards were social dances in the very real sense of being society-forming dances. Modern rock is crowd-forming, rather than society-forming, and courtesy plays no part in it.

However, dancing is an important and probably necessary part of social life. It shapes the body rhythms and trains the ears of those who engage in it, and changes in the dance-culture will lead of their own accord to changes in the rhythmical organisation of music – even the music of the concert hall. This is what we witnessed in the 19th century, when gypsy rhythms affected the music of Brahms (explicitly, in works like the G minor piano quartet, but implicitly in many of the other chamber works, songs and concerti), and when the waltz exerted an ubiquitous fascination that was to begin with Schubert's drawing-room waltzes for piano, and to culminate in Ravel's monumental *La Valse* for orchestra.

This is one of the factors that must be borne in mind when we consider the relation between serious and popular music today. People have become used to the ostinato rhythms of pop, which throb in the background of life and shape the expectations of all of us, like it or not. It is hard to attract modern audiences to music in which rhythm is internally generated; comparatively easy to attract them to music with an ostinato propulsion, regardless of its melodic or harmonic invention. Hence the popularity of John Adams, whose 'Short Ride in a Fast Machine' typifies a new kind of ostinato writing, with the melodic instruments assigned essentially percussive tasks, and with continual repetition of elemental rhythmical cells. For the pop-trained ear this music is easy to listen to, since its rhythmic structure does not have to be deciphered through listening but is imposed by a regular external emphasis. Composers used to be wary of 'the tyranny of the bar-line'; in Adams, however, the tyranny is accepted, as a benign dictatorship which gives us all what we want.

Others, responding like Adams to the new experience of rhythm as a *drive*, have nevertheless attempted to break the tyranny of the bar-line through syncopation and rhythmical sub-division. An example is Michael Torke, in his 'Colour' works. Here strings and wind are again used percussively, but with a kind of jagged and Beethovenian obsessiveness, hammering home the down-beat. Still, however, I would say that the rhythm has entered this music from a point outside it. The melodic phrases and altered diatonic harmonies are as it were swelled up by the rhythm, as by a wind, so as to sound bigger, grander, fuller than they are.

I don't intend that as criticism, but merely as a phenomenological description. But it bears on the controversy surrounding modern music, between those who adhere to the old demands of the tonal tradition, and those who make a point of defying it. When this controversy is rehearsed in the pages of learned journals it tends to focus on the concept of tonality, conceived as a melodic and harmonic system, and characterised by the fundamentally goal-directed nature of the harmonic and melodic expectations of the tonal idiom. Rhythm is usually left out of the picture. In fact, however, tonality is also a rhythmical system – one which depends on the bar-line and also gives sense to the bar-line as an organic outgrowth of the musical development.

Much modernist music is rhythmless – not just in the sense of lacking metrical divisions, time-signatures and so on – but in the sense of lacking a pulse that survives the individual note or sound that produces it. The inspiration here comes partly from Stockhausen, whose music shifts great blocks of sound through musical space, with the same indifference to human life and bodily sensations as a slave-minder building a pyramid. If you were to introduce rhythm into a piece like *Gruppen*, for example, it would have to be an external rhythm, like a pop-ostinato, laid on top of the musical structure but generated outside it. For the music itself has no enduring pulse; the emphasis generated within one episode does not survive to the next, and therefore cannot combine with it in a dance step. There is a curious parallel here, between Stockhausen and John Adams: both think of rhythm in ostinato terms, the one therefore rejecting it, as an extra-musical device, the other accepting it as the sole organizing principle of a musical surface that in all other respects is wholly monotonous.

The evident contrast with this is the music of Messiaen, in which the bar-line is infected with new life by rhythms that are entirely melodically generated – as in the *Turangalîla* Symphony. In this kind of writing you see that the bar-line is not a frame imposed on the music, but an order extracted from it. The rhythm is generated by the energy that ties each note to its neighbour, as in a spontaneous dance. The bar-line is, as it were, precipitated out of this energy. It is the effect, and not the cause, of the rhythmical order.

However, it is not Messiaen whom I wish to consider in this paper: his case is too special to give confidence in what I wish to say. Rather I want to look back at the origin of modern music, in Wagner's *Tristan und Isolde*, and to suggest that the tonal and rhythmic organisation that we witness in that work are two aspects of a single musical process. Wagner is not often thought of as a rhythmic innovator, or as a particularly rhythmical composer. That is because we have fallen for the external, ostinato conception of rhythm, and to a great measure lost sight of the origins of rhythm in the musical line. In fact, however, Wagner is one of the great rhythmists. This is so in spite of the fact, and also because of the fact, that Wagner hardly ever uses percussion as a rhythm-generating device. The timpani play an enormous role in *Tristan*, but it is a melodic role, consisting largely of prolonged tremolandi which swell the melodic line and suggest huge reserves of unexplored emotion in the depths. And the other instruments of the orchestra are used melodically rather than percussively, even in the most frenetic passages such as the scene in which Tristan tears the bandages from his wound, and the music enters a kind of rhythmic catastrophe as its strives to keep pace with his delirium.

Beethoven's architecture, in works like the fifth symphony, the violin concerto and the third piano concerto, depends upon repetition of rhythmic motives which can be detached from the melodies that first impress them on the listener, and reduced to purely metrical form. Yet they are melodically generated. The four note motive that sets the first movement of the fifth symphony in motion is not hammered out but sung, with the G-E flat interval absolutely integral to the effect. Even the repeated notes on the timpani that open the violin concerto owe their reverberation in the memory to the melodic and harmonic sequence that they prefigure, which gives to them a half-cadential character.

Wagner's motives in *Tristan* have pronounced rhythmical contours, but, unlike the Beethoven examples, their emphasis is rarely on the downbeat. Consider the motive sometimes known as the 'look', which sets the Prelude in motion, after the interrupted cadence on to F major. This establishes a complex rhythm in 6/8 time, with a fractured triplet followed by a crotchet-quaver sigh. The melodic line here, and the chromatic movement in the bass which lifts the harmony from F major to G major, endow the rhythmic pattern of this phrase with a kind of completeness. This is a rhythm that has been 'sung out', and which henceforth bears the memory of the phrases that sang it. Wagner promptly repeats it, incorporating it into no less than five subsequent motives, which it draws together with the original 'look' to form a continuous sequence.

In the classical style the closures imposed by tonal melody and diatonic harmony are aligned with rhythmical closures reinforced by bar-lines. In *Tristan* all three forms of closure are minimised or avoided entirely: for they are symbols of a law-governed order that passion has undermined. Hence the motives that take up the rhythmic organisation of the 'look' involve ties across bar-lines, off-beat accents, and the ubiquitous fracture in the triplet, that together create a rhythmic profile that cannot be understood apart from the melodic pulse from which it derives. The prelude to *Tristan* shows how the tyranny of the bar-line can be escaped: by making the bar-line into the effect, rather than the cause, of the rhythmic organisation.

At the same time, the music of *Tristan* is intensely rhythmical. Motives and melodic phrases have a pronounced metrical organisation, which makes them recognizable through changes of spacing, harmony and tessitura. Thus many of the motives appear in compressed or expanded form, with intervals and harmonies altered, but nevertheless retaining their identity by virtue of their sharp rhythmic profile. But the rhythm has been, as it were, internalised: it remains locked within the motive itself, part of its inner movement. This movement may spread into the surrounding musical space – as the 'look' motive spreads its movement through the Prelude to Act I – but is not derived from any external metrical pulse. It is generated from within the musical movement, and would be inconceivable apart from the tonal organisation of that movement, which endows it with its onward-going flow.

The use of rhythm in *Tristan* reminds us of the fact that rhythm belongs not merely to the context of dancing, but also to that of speech. And it is in speech that we are most clearly presented with rhythmic organisation that is *derived* from the movement, rather than imposed on it. One of the most remarkable developments within the sphere of pop is the so-called 'rap' artist, who speaks toneless rhyming prose along the groove of a relentless percussive rhythm, so cancelling all natural speech-rhythms and making a kind of machine-like parody of human discourse. This is an extreme form of the ostinato experience, in which speech rhythms themselves are dismembered and fragmented by the externally generated beat. It offers a vivid reminder of the fact that musical rhythms, like speech-rhythms, are, in their primary occurrence, internal to the musical form, and inseparable from the pauses and closures required by the needs of expression.

In *Tristan* all this is made abundantly clear by the fact that the tonal language has been bent entirely to the task of giving expression to inner states of mind, so capturing their climaxes, compulsions and hesitations. Often Janácek is given credit for being the first composer to build speech rhythms into his melodic line. It seems to me, however, that speech rhythms have been part of phrasing in classic music from the earliest days, and that the conscious attempt to give them musical form began with Wagner, not Janácek. Wagner himself discusses the matter in *Opera and Drama*, referring to the accents that are natural to the spoken language as underpinning the musical divisions within the bar. (See *Oper und Drama, dritter Theil: Dichtkunst und Tonkunst.*) His use of *Stabreim* arose directly from his search for a language that could be sung out without losing the inflections of natural speech. And I suspect that there might be a useful contrast to be made between composers whose rhythmic organisation primarily reflects dance patterns, and those for whom speech patterns are more important. Tchaikovsky, Dvořák and Stravinsky belong to the first kind; Mussorgsky, Wagner, Janáček and Schoenberg to the second. (In Stravinsky's Les Noces, for example, the composer uses nonsense syllables, precisely in order to reconstitute speech-rhythms as dance-rhythms. In Stravinsky it is not words that give the meaning of the dance, but dance that gives the meaning of the words.)

Mention of Schoenberg brings me to the issue of atonal music. Schoenberg's atonalism is often thought to have arisen in the course of harmonic experiments, designed to free the composer from the cloying quality of post-Wagnerian chromaticism. But it is more appropriately seen as an experiment in rhythm. Atonalism involves, in Schoenberg, a radical repudiation of dance-rhythm and an adoption of speech-rhythm as the fundamental organising principle of the melodic line. This is evident not merely in *Sprechgesang* but also in the way in which the spoken word infects the melodic line and imposes its own accents, climaxes and closures. The instrumentation and harmony of a work like *Pierrot Lunaire* are dictated in part by the desire to generate speech-like rhythms in all the instrumental voices. Tonal harmony compels voices to move together, to magnetize each other, to work towards the same points of closure and stasis – as in a dance. Hence, however much speech rhythm may inspire the melodic line, a reminiscence of dance rhythm will inhabit the harmony. This is very clearly apparent in *Tristan*, and in the 'look' motive referred to earlier. The onward movement of this motive is harmonically driven, through the chromatic bass-line, and the effect of the motive is to combine the speech-rhythm of the melodic line, with a kind of 'dancing along' in the harmony – like the sing-song-dance of the Greek tragic chorus (a comparison explicitly made by Wagner in *Opera and Drama*.)

In order to free the music entirely from this dance-like togetherness, Schoenberg pulls the harmony apart, so that what we hear is a simultaneity of voices rather than a single chord. The later development of the serial technique likewise has a pronounced rhythmical meaning. The serialisation of the pitch sequence permits a kind of poly-rhythmic structure, in which accents in the various voices seldom coincide, and the unified chorus gives way to a conversation. (Examples of interest: the chorus of the Israelites wandering in the desert in *Moses and Aaron* – contrast the flat and ineffective dance rhythms that accompany the worship of the golden calf.)

In *The Aesthetics of Music* I argue that the musical experience should be construed on the model of dancing: that is to say, a sympathetic movement, in which you 'move with' the music, by imagining movement in the music itself. I suggest that this explains both the delight that we take in musical form, and also its moral character. By moving with the music you shape your emotional repertoire, much as you do through manners, courtesies and formalities. You are learning the process of 'fit' between yourself and an idealized social world. I believe that Plato had an inkling of this, in his account of the various modes of Greek music.

It seems to me, therefore, that rhythmic organisation is absolutely fundamental to musical meaning. I have no doubt that the externalised rhythm of much contemporary pop is not merely anti-musical; it is also demoralising. It is inviting people to move in crowd-like rather than conversation-like ways. You do not 'move with' rhythm of this kind; you surrender to it, are overwhelmed by it. You lose yourself in it, as in a drug. The classical tradition often uses ostinato – but almost invariably in a form that arises from the internal organisation of the musical line. The ostinato rhythms in the Bartók piano sonata, for example, have no reality apart from the sharpened harmonies and emphatic melodic line that produce them. You do not lose yourself in these rhythms: rather you discover something *other* than yourself – an idealized peasant community in touch with the soil.

John Adams, Michael Torke and others have reacted against the official modernism that has prevailed in our concert halls – and understandably. Although they have brought music back to tonal harmonies and diatonic melodies – albeit of a simple kind – the real impulse behind their experiments has been rhythmical. The Darmstadt orthodoxy effectively killed off rhythmical organisation as an intrinsic feature of the musical line. People can listen to Stockhausen's *Gruppen*, for example, and move 'along with' it and even be moved by it. But the fundamental experience on which all listening (as opposed to hearing) depends – the experience of rhythm – is simply absent from Stockhausen's block-like sounds. It is absent too from the works of James Macmillan, from most of the works of Harrison Birtwistle, and from much else that now forms the official modern repertoire.

But I believe that Adams and Torke have got things the wrong way round. They are addressing our need for rhythm by *adding* rhythm to melodic lines and harmonies that do not have the strength to generate rhythm out of their own inner movement. The rhythm is pumped in from outside, not breathed out by the melody. Once again we are in the vicinity of those 'crowd' experiences that dominate the world of pop. The real listening tradition depends upon composers who invite us to join in rhythms that are intrinsic to the melodic and harmonic life of their music.

There are many such composers writing today –
David Matthews, for example, in his string quartets and

symphonies; John Borstlap in 'Psyche'; Michael Berkeley in his organ concerto; Oliver Knussen in his two operas on childhood themes, *Higgledy-Piggledy-Pop* and *Where the Wild Things Are*. And these works are primarily tonal, illustrating the thesis that tonality is a *rhythmical* system, arising when voices 'move with' each other, as in a dance. They illustrate both the depth and the importance of the controversy surrounding musical modernism. This is not a controversy about harmonic systems only; it is primarily a controversy about the nature of listening, about the role of music in the shaping of our emotions, and about the connection between music and life.

Part 2

Music as
a social
and spiritual
happening

WHAT IS THE CORE BUSINESS OF AN ORCHESTRA?

PROGRAMMING FOR A SYMPHONY ORCHESTRA IN A MULTI-CULTURAL CONTEXT
Leo Samama

How does an orchestra behave and what does it programme between governmental and local regulations, shifting cultural patterns, political pressure from local communities and the central government with regard to artistic content and socio-cultural significance?

Programming an orchestra is strongly defined by the mission an organisation has set itself, by the necessity of box office income, by the artistic standards of musicians and board alike, by the wishes of individual conductors and soloists, and also by the more overall repertoire planning as formulated by the orchestra with regard to subscription series on the one hand and external obligations on the other. One may ask oneself whether an institution like a symphony orchestra should define its cultural obligations with regard to a changing culture, or whether even in a changing culture one should accept that a symphony orchestra in the main will be a given institute with a given repertoire.

But political regulations do require the symphony orchestras to consider performing for a multi-cultural audience and even engaging musicians from the ever-growing group of 'new Dutchmen'. Several orchestras in the Netherlands did try to bridge the gap between their usual performances for mainly white people (and I mean 'white by complexion' as much as 'white of hair'...) and the changing cultural composition of the population within the boundaries of their cities. For example, the Residentie Orkest and the Rotterdams Philharmonisch Orkest organised concerts for Turkish popular singers and symphony orchestra, with either newly made arrangements or ones adapted specifically for symphony orchestra.

Thus the former orchestra engaged a popular Turkish pop singer, Nilüfer, with her band and had her most famous songs arranged by a local composer for symphony orchestra. The concert was announced and ticketed as part of a larger festival with the help of a local Turkish cultural organisation. Some 1,700 young Turkish people attended this production.

They loved the pop music of course, but were – happily enough – as much enchanted by the contemporary Turkish music, which was programmed as a curtain raiser. Even the musicians of the orchestra enjoyed the festive atmosphere, the attractive music and the enthusiastic reception. This example is one of many in a multi-cultural cross-border context.

One could also mention examples of cross-genre or crossover projects within a single culture, as for example pop concerts with symphony orchestra, or (silent) film and music projects, symphonic jazz with soloists or big band and so forth. Again the Residentie Orkest has had some quite interesting experiences with such crossovers, both in the concert hall and in open-air concerts. The first question to be raised is: why should an orchestra programme what is not the core business of this particular body of musicians?

Part of this question is, of course: what *is* the core business of an orchestra? The second question is whether an orchestra should present what exists already (Beethoven and Brahms for example, or Pfitzner and Elgar, or even Boulez and Andriessen), or whether it should first of all partake in innovation, in a new repertoire. A sequel to this question is: should one cross cultural and/or social borders, or should one recognize the primordial fact that a symphony orchestra is a symphony orchestra, and not a rock band or a Hindu ensemble? Let's start with the first question, which is indeed a bit of a tricky one, as the actual symphony orchestra has proven not to be a fixed body of musicians. New instruments were added during the 19th and 20th centuries, new repertoire – albeit purely symphonic – was created over the years and is still being created every day. However, the general practice shows that by far the most orchestras prefer as core business the classical-romantic symphonic repertoire, from Haydn to Prokofjev, Beethoven to Shostakovich, and Schubert to Britten.

The more orchestras compete with each other on pure quality and sheer sound (as triggered by the recording and CD industry over the last three decades), and the more this happens in a global context and with the media as an extra means of exposure (how does 'my' orchestra sound compared to the Berlin Philharmonic or the San Francisco Symphony?), the more often conductors and orchestra managements alike prefer to specialize in the well-known (and therefore comparable) past and not the unknown (hence incomparable) future, that is, in the *canon* of music making and not in innovations.

The moral obligation of an orchestra towards music, of any musician in fact towards music, is: exposing scores by making them sound. Under the present circumstances this will therefore be restricted to playing what is known, preferably doing so better than others. However, one extra question remains: what is a better performance? Is this a technical or a musical phenomenon? And hasn't one lost a sixth sense for the difference between these two? Especially since the rise of the modern gramophone recording industry, its sophisticated editing techniques using tapes and nowadays computers, and the possibilities of comparing scores of recorded interpretations, technical perfection in performance seems to have become more important than the perfection of expression. The second question is whether an orchestra should resemble the Rijksmuseum, with its famous old masters, or the Stedelijk Museum, with its contemporary art. Should an orchestra reflect in its programmes the culture which is *generated* in our own times (music now, actual music, contemporary music) or the culture, which is the subject of *reflection* in our times (any music of all times and all cultures)? Which is socially most commonly accepted (those ever present large numbers...)? And which brings a boost to the box office? Is it the marketing department of cultural organisations, which should do the programming, or is it the city council, or should one stick to high artistic standards (define 'artistic standards', please!)? One might imagine that as the artistic manager of an orchestra I personally would prefer the classiest and artistically most elevated solution. But I don't. An orchestra, as I mentioned before, should mirror today's culture in the broadest sense of the word, with one essential restriction. It should never deny what it is, and always will be: a symphony orchestra, and not a band, a dance orchestra or a large ensemble. This means: whatever you do, you should always be aware that the orchestra is an *orchestra*.

These reflections bring us to day-to-day practice, and to our day-to-day partners: the board and the management, the chief conductor, the artistic committee (on behalf of the orchestra), the promoter (if another than the orchestra itself), the audience, the critics, the record companies, the touring agencies, guest conductors and soloists, the government, the city council and sponsors. Each of these may have their own wishes, often even demands. Very often these demands are to some extent connected to finances, subventions, sponsoring, and box office income.

At the end of the day, decisions are the result of endless negotiations and numerous compromises. And too often especially politicians express much more advanced ideas than they are willing to finance through subventions or extra financial impulses. Thus the inclusion of the Residentie Orkest in a prestigious Hindustani festival was aborted by the unwillingness of the city council to support this financially, while at the same time they expressed the (political and cultural) importance of our plans....
Part of the day-to-day practice therefore is also defined by the results of our undertakings, not only in relation to councils and sponsors, but also to the box office results and the envisaged changes in the composition of our audiences.

And in this respect, I am not very optimistic. It seems that cultural institutions are asked for a multi-cultural mission in order to back up political views and attract new voters.
Of course, when we organize children's concerts and at least 50% of the children in our concert hall are 'new Dutch' (Hindustani, Moroccan, Algerian, Turkish, Surinamese), we do experience a certain feeling of fulfilment. Especially when the evaluations by the schools indicate that these children like the shows no less than Dutch children. But will these new Dutchmen come to our concert hall for the regular traditional concerts? I doubt it sincerely. At least, if they do, it will only be in very small numbers. But then, various gospels started with only a handful of believers...

Therefore, I personally will go on trying to bring music to the attention of the diverse population of the Netherlands. Either by inviting new audiences to rehearsals or concerts, or by organising special features for them as the ones mentioned above, and also by organising open-air concerts at various locations. Even when the results of these ventures will not altogether change the world, they will bring people together, and they will bring other cultures and other musical genres under the attention of the professional musicians' orchestras and ensembles.

To bring this short reflection to an end, I'd like to add some thoughts as a composer. Mozart, Bach, Beethoven, and Brahms were very much aware of the popular music of their times, and they were able to partake in the important osmosis between higher and lower culture (if one would like to call it that way). Today's composers too should try to combine their sometimes quite inhumanly high standards with regard to their compositional products with a more down-to-earth sense of reality concerning our changing world and its cultural implications.

Instead of boasting Euro-centrism ('our culture has a higher grade of development...'), some real interest in other cultures – not as something exotic, not as a funny 'couleur locale', but in their techniques and the meanings behind these techniques – would enhance our own art, and would give it a better chance to survive the ever growing pressures of modern-day commercialism and internationalism. I am not referring to cultural integration – one should hold on to one's own cultural identity –, but to real understanding and respect. Cultural integration is a dangerous way of being forced to lose one's own cultural identity. Understanding and respect really bring people together.

The ways to the future are manifold, and every culture, every genre, every expression of art should partake in the search for a world of mutual acceptance and understanding, a world without envy or war, a world driven by ethics and not only by money.

THE CONCERT HALL
CAN BE A GATEWAY
TO 'OTHERNESS'

REMAKING THE *TEMENOS*: THE CONCERT HALL AS THE SPIRITUAL CENTRE OF THE COMMUNITY
Peter Davison

1 Karen Armstrong,
  A History of God,
  William Heinemann Ltd.,
  London 1993.

I am the artistic consultant to Manchester's Bridgewater Hall, a 2000-seat, acoustically-designed venue for classical music. I obtained that position a few years before the hall's public opening in September 1996, and since that time, I have often had cause to reflect on what is the real value of a concert hall in a post-industrial European city. In this essay, I want to explore the possibility that such a building can in some way function as the spiritual centre of a complex, contemporary community. I do this with some reluctance, since I claim neither to be a high priest of music, nor that concert halls can replace more conventional religious establishments. Nonetheless, the idea that cultural organisations may assist the spiritual well-being of the communities to which they belong is a matter for serious consideration, not least because the more traditional means of binding us together have lost their effectiveness.

Our prevailing European culture is secular, and any consensus about religious practice has gradually declined in the last two-hundred years to the point where the loss is rarely contested. Formal ritual, that is the emotional heart of any religion, is not a regular part of most people's lives. Baptisms, marriages and funerals are the most likely occasions when an average person might find themselves participating in religion, but these are treated more like personal landmarks. They no longer express any real sense of unity with the divine or acknowledge the affirmative presence of a wider community.

In addition, the faith which might have given meaning to such ceremonies has long ago withered into superstition or empty convention. Karen Armstrong in her formidable text, *A History of God*[1], points out that a religion which has become dogmatic and over-rational inevitably declines. The binding presence of divinity, experienced through ritual, requires an emotional surrender alien to the reasoning mind. Once the ritual is emptied, as *logos* replaces *mythos*, the effectiveness of a religion dwindles. The authority of Christianity in the West

57

has been undermined by the rise of science as the measure of truth. Scepticism has eroded the power of Christian symbols, and consequently the bonds of community have also been loosened. The rise in personal neurosis, fanaticism and fundamentalism, Armstrong suggests, is directly related to the collapse of ritual at the heart of our communities.

It is a point which has an unlikely solidarity with the early work of Friedrich Nietzsche, who condemned the rationalism and progressiveness of what he called the 'Socratic' outlook in his brilliant study, *The Birth of Tragedy*[2]. In this essay, Nietzsche blames the death of Greek Tragedy, itself a ritual of catharsis, on an historical and critical mode of perception, which replaced the more irrational aesthetic responses, which he believed Tragedy demands.

Nietzsche suggests, with an obvious debt to Schopenhauer and Wagner, that only great music has the power to stir the feelings which were once the province of Greek tragedy. Those feelings were, for Nietzsche, our direct experience of the world-will, the moving force of creation in all its dark power. When we listen to great music, Nietzsche says, we are overwhelmed by a feeling of beauty, even when it expresses pain, grief or sadness. This moment of transcendence offers meaning to our lives and purges us of the horror and uncertainty, which is the common lot of Man.

> Both [music and tragic myth] transfigure a region in whose chords of delight dissonance, as well as the terrible image of the world, charmingly fade away; they both play with the sting of pleasure, trusting to their extremely powerful magical arts; both use this play to justify the existence even of the 'worst world'.[3]

If we agree with Nietzsche, and I am inclined to, then music has a unique role to play as a substitute for religious ritual in a secular age, and an awareness of this must inform how we programme our major concert halls and relate to our audiences.

The era of the CD-player has displaced a very significant aspect of music, namely that it should be experienced 'live' and with a group of listeners. In this more traditional context, the paradox is apparent that music remains profoundly intimate for each individual, despite the presence of others. This is the source of music's ritualistic power. When we listen, we feel a range of emotions, from despair to ecstasy, but there is more to it than simply a narrative of feelings. In symphonic music, oppositions and tensions naturally move towards resolution and synthesis, offering us the possibility of experiencing profound meaning, even when, as Nietzsche has indicated, the music's emotional content is extremely negative. By sharing this cathartic experience with others, we are also reassured that our inner world is not one of incoherence and solipsistic isolation. Quite simply, we feel more whole and less alone.

2 Friedrich Nietzsche, *The Birth of Tragedy* (originally *Die Geburt der Tragödie*, Leipzig 1872, revised 1874, 1886), English trans. Shaun Whiteside, ed. Michael Tanner, for Penguin Books, London 1993.

3 Nietzsche, *The Birth of Tragedy*, Chapter 25.

Music, by moving seamlessly from the general to the particular, the communal to the personal, helps us to define our selfhood, while also holding out a vision of community to which we can aspire.

The sceptic will argue that these ideas are plausible, but illusory, since, in our contemporary society, classical music has been stripped of its spiritual meaning by being sold in the same way as soap powder and motor cars. It can no longer fulfil an elevated function, as it has become just another consumer-item, another form of leisure, competing for our money and attention. The evidence that classical music has been consumerised is indisputable. The hyperbolae of marketing jargon are found in most concert hall literature, subtly falsifying the true quality of 'live' musical experience by reducing it to an elite form of relaxation. This situation has often demoralised those composers treading the path of moral integrity, and many have sought a quasi-monastic refuge in academia, hiding from vulgarity and capitalist excess, often behind the impenetrable facade of modernist orthodoxy. It is a legitimate point of view, but one which abandons the notion that high culture can be transformative and provide a unifying force for society.

In more recent times, a pervasive *ennui* with consumerism has emerged with the realisation of the damage it has done both to us and the environment. There has been a resurgence of interest in spiritual matters, and from beneath the veneer of marketing jargon and 'business-speak', music is re-emerging as a potent spiritual force. Because music cannot be adequately described in words and because it speaks directly to the soul, it has resisted the attempt to disenchant our culture more successfully than other art-forms. Consequently, as our culture has hesitantly begun to revive, concert halls have been an important factor in this process of regeneration.

If this view seems implausible, then one needs only examine the recent history of our larger towns and cities. The immediate post-war period was a time when the spiritual life was unfashionable and its connection to our culture was systematically severed. Making the arts into a form of leisure (or, at best, some kind of social therapy) reinforced the idea that all human activity could be explained in terms of social, economic and political theories. Those musicians who sought to resist this utilitarian approach often resorted to revolutionary ideology and radical theorisation as a defence. Communism or capitalism, whatever the label, the effect was the same; a denial of the true nature of Man as a feeling and spiritual being. This objectification of human identity justified the barbarism of those Utopian dreamers of the 1960s, who destroyed the souls of many of our European cities, places such as Dresden, Birmingham and Rotterdam. They unwittingly finished the work of destruction begun by the bombs of the

4 John Myerscough,
*The Economic Impor-
tance of the Arts on
Mersey side*, Policy
Studies Institute,
London 1982.

Second World War. With fanatical excess, the city-planners created the now crumbling concrete wastelands, which offend the eye and crush the spirit. Thankfully such buildings are at last attracting the attention of the demolition men.

It seems hard to look back to that time and accept that much of this urban planning was idealistic, but it was then popular to believe that our past was a tyranny to be shrugged off. A kind of madness pertains in such ideological climates. In the immediate post-war period, modernist idealism cast out common sense. Boulez felt justified in inviting us to burn down the opera houses. His was a revolutionary posture; one which he has subsequently recanted as a stalwart of Bayreuth. His polemic still haunts him, however, since he was mistakenly arrested as a suspected terrorist in Switzerland some time after the 9/11 calamity.

In the later decades of the 20th century, it was slowly recognised by the town planners that there was a human dimension to urban regeneration and that the arts and culture had a role to play. The ground-breaking work by John Myerscough and the Policy Studies Institute[4] in the eighties made an argument for funding the arts entirely based on their economic outputs, such as job-creation, wealth-generation and tourism, but little mention was made of the arts for their own sake, as if this was embarrassing; hankering after an outmoded belief in the value of high art. Such studies may have been valid attempts to preserve funding for the arts in a hostile climate, but they played into the hands of bureaucrats, which could now set economic and commercial criteria in measuring the effectiveness of public support. It is a fashion on the wane, thank goodness, but much of this materialist rhetoric still persists in the corridors of many government departments.

In the nineties, the importance of the arts in regenerating our major European cities became more and more evident. The new Guggenheim Museum in Bilbao is one of the most striking examples. In such cases, the investment is justified by the arts' contribution to local and regional identity. That our communities are made up of people with a common culture, not just a common desire for wealth, seems absurdly obvious, but there is still much materialist thinking around, encouraged by accountants and management consultants, who find the ambiguities of human nature too inconvenient. But the truth is undeniable. The practice of the arts and the buildings that house them are the best expression of community that we have.

Despite the influence of countless spurious economic and political theories, good human instincts have prevailed. In Great Britain, over the last twenty years, the building of high quality concert halls for symphonic music has been a symbol of revival for our major provincial cities. However, the design of these halls has reflected our ambivalence about the spiritual function of the arts. Cardiff, capital of Wales, a nation of musicians and poets, led the way with St. David's Hall in 1982; a fine auditorium, but the building offers almost no public face and is located above a shopping mall. In 1991 came two new halls. Birmingham's Symphony Hall was a fruit of Sir Simon Rattle's tenure in the City. It is another grand, space-age auditorium, but once again lost in the mall-like complex of the National Exhibition Centre. Glasgow's Royal Hall arrived in Scotland, sadly a rather austere edifice next to a department store, but it was still born of the same surge of civic and regional idealism as the others. (We see the same pattern in other halls such as the Barbican in London or the Vredenburg in Utrecht, which are both buried in the bunker of Mammon. Such buildings seem reluctant to declare themselves as public space.)

It was in 1996 that Manchester opened its own new concert hall as a home for the famous Hallé orchestra, and it was the first of the major new halls in Britain to separate itself fully from the shopping precinct. The Bridgewater Hall's appearance is not especially bold, but it does declare that it is public space; a glass frontage and ship-like prow emerge from behind the modernist grey cladding that form its outer walls. The design of Renton Howard Wood Levine had the confidence to invite the public in. So at last, there was some visible recognition of what had been true all along, namely that these new concert halls in Britain were symbols of the transformation of our troubled Victorian cities, providing a spiritual core and source of identity. These were places where the community could gather to renew its sense of unity and creative possibility, where the community could reconnect with its historic identity, now reshaped for the modern world.

Should we be surprised that the enclosed space of the concert hall should serve this spiritual purpose? No, for just about every religion cites the need for a core of inner stillness as the prerequisite of authentic spiritual experience, and at the communal level this has traditionally been expressed by the centrality of religious buildings in human settlements. For the ancient Greeks, the temple was the still centre, and in the medieval European city, it was the cathedral. Music has always played a special role in animating these quiet places and providing an appropriate atmosphere for religious ceremonies, be it the meditative undulation of plainchant or the exuberant jubilation of a Bach cantata. In our own time, if concert halls can uphold the spiritual values of high art, they will question the validity of the prevailing consumerist culture. The concert hall can be a remaking of the *temenos*, the frame of sacred space found in ancient Greek temples, so that once again, at the heart of our urban communities, there can be a place of purification, a gateway to 'otherness', where our sense of reality can be transformed to renew the moral and social order.

This link between modern concert halls and the structure of the Greek temple is not a fanciful coincidence. The Bridgewater Hall was designed to be remote from the world, although located in Manchester's city centre. The auditorium is physically and acoustically isolated from its surroundings. It rests upon over 100 springs, which prevent vibration intruding from outside. Busy traffic rumbles around the hall, yet the silence of the auditorium is palpable and deliberate. The feeling of stillness in so vast a space encourages religious awe, reinforced by the massive array of organ pipes that clings to the back wall and the numinous sheen of the hall's warm acoustics. There are no overt religious symbols, but people instinctively feel that this is a special space. And indeed, when a marvellous concert is happening there, the intense concentration and engagement of 2000 people, perhaps on one performer, is as striking as any religious ceremony. Some of the best concerts I have heard at the hall have been of religious music. The fourteen-second hiatus that was sustained at the end of a performance of Duruflé's *Requiem* illustrates the point. The hall was built for such poignant silences.

Manchester was the cradle of the industrial revolution and among the first cities to confront the problems of the post-industrial period. It has deep-rooted, long-standing problems of urban deprivation and physical decline. This may cause some people to feel uneasy: should a city be building a lavish £42m concert venue, while some of its communities are wretched with poverty, violence and drugs? Some will also feel the dark spectre of the Nuremberg rallies at work, that I am advocating mass hysteria, music as a bourgeois narcotic, instead of facing grim social realities. The civic cult contains all the dangers of brash populism and sentimentalised camaraderie, but these should not deter the effort to create icons of renewal, for the alternative is despair and cynicism.

In any case, truly great music has the power to rescue us, because it can transcend such pitfalls. I am reminded of the wonderful satirical novel by Günter Grass, *The Tin Drum*[5], in which the eternal child, Oskar, disrupts a Nazi rally by banging a waltz-rhythm on his toy drum behind the speaker's podium. The irresistible force of delight overwhelms the dreary, pompous marches of the militarists and the entire crowd starts to dance. The furious demagogue loses his grip upon the assembled masses. Silencing the fanatics and those who wish to rob us of wonder and delight is one of the main goals of concert programming. We should recognise that sometimes pure joy is the best antidote to cynicism and evil.

There are those who will argue that Western classical music does not possess this purity, tainted as it is by the imperial past and corrupt consumer society from which it has sprung. Music clearly has an ethical dimension, because it manifests itself in the real world. It can be abused or misappropriated like

5 Günter Grass, *The Tin Drum* (originally *Die Blechtrommel*, Luchterhand, Neuwied am Rhein 1959), English trans. Ralph Manheim, Penguin Books, London, many reprints since 1965.

anything else. We should certainly avoid the errors of Richard Strauss and Wilhelm Furtwängler, who failed to recognise that their beloved German music had been stolen by opportunists. In such a circumstance, the corrupting force should certainly be resisted. But great music is able to transcend the ethical flaws of the society which spawns it, because the meanings that are attributed to it by politicians and politically-motivated theorists have little to do with its function as art. For this reason, concert halls should avoid being a source of polemic and, as much as possible, strive to depoliticise the public space. Great music should provide an inviolable inner realm, which sets a boundary to the ordinary world.

I want briefly to summarise the context of planning for the modern concert hall, before going on to discuss the more practical challenges of programming. There are four key points:

> Great classical music provides the much needed emotional power of ritual in a secular society; one which opens a window to the spiritual realm.

> Concert halls have iconic status as public buildings, signalling to the population that they belong to a community embodied in bricks and mortar. The communal experience of great music reinforces this sense of collectivity.

> Good new concert halls raise musical standards, enhancing the cosmopolitan image of a city and stirring the population's own creative ambitions.

> Programming must not be political or polemical. It must transcend the divisions and decadence of the times, so that the concert hall can successfully serve its iconic and transcendental functions.

The Bridgewater Hall's programme policy is democratic in the sense that we are answerable directly to the public through the discipline of the marketplace. This means that an artistic vision develops as a dialogue between the planners and the public. It is essential that we create the perception that The Bridgewater Hall is a dynamic place to be and where people expect marvellous things happen. This is not populism, for the core of our activity is high culture and includes up to 150 classical music concerts per year, but the programme is 'audience-aware'. That audience is anyone who seeks to hear the best music in a high quality environment. This dialogue with the public makes sense, not solely as a response to commercial pressure, but exactly because The Bridgewater Hall is an iconic presence in the city; acting as a bridge between old and new, providing a symbol of hope. We try to raise people's sights about standards, about creative possibility.

We also reassure the public that the established canon of the classical repertoire has a secure place in the culture. We are not progressive in some artificial way, but nor can we cocoon ourselves from social change. It is necessarily and willingly a pragmatic approach.

I want to say unequivocally that the symphonic tradition is at the very heart of the Bridgewater Hall's programme. It was the reason for the hall's construction; a recognition of the importance of orchestral music-making in the city for over 150 years. Orchestral music is one of the crucial badges of the city's identity, and the hall was intended to secure the future of the Hallé orchestra by giving it a new home.

While the conventional wisdom is that this rewards only a small group of classical music fanatics from a narrow social group, the truth is that audiences in Manchester come from a wide range of backgrounds. Sometimes 10,000 people per week attend the hall to hear orchestral music. It is in the population's blood, symbolising a tradition of civic pride and achievement.

The existence of a wide range of social and ethnic groups in the City does not lead us to dilute our commitment to Western classical music. There are other venues that can serve those communities better. We happily enter into a dialogue with such groups and there is a commitment to programme music from other cultures, because it represents the best of its kind and has the potential to appeal to a broad audience. Such concerts throw the Western classical programme into relief and bring new audiences into the building. We suffer no guilt from our strong advocacy of Western culture, for it is not a supremacist position. Symphonic music is just an important part of Manchester's culture and heritage. We champion our identity with the same enthusiasm as would an Indian in Mumbai or a Jamaican in Kingston. We are currently expanding our programme of jazz and world music, in response to increasing public interest, but we are doing this collaboratively with well-informed and well-connected promoters rather than pretending we are experts.

I want also unequivocally to say that we believe in the idea that some music is better than other music.

We make value judgements all the time about what kind of programme we want to put across. Broad public interest alone is not enough for us to promote an artist or ensemble. We want a quality programme, which means the best performers performing the best music, and that criterion is not genre-specific. A categorisation that might lead us to say all pop music or jazz is less good than all classical music would be crudely inadequate.

We want the best in all fields, be they brass bands, children's choirs, swing bands or organists. We are not heavily judgemental; we will try things out, experiment occasionally, give the benefit of the doubt, but we are quick to learn from mistakes. We do make them and need the courage to go on making them.

I want to conclude by saying a few words about our attitude to programming contemporary music in the classical tradition. It is a highly risky business for a large hall, but we feel a strong responsibility to encourage new music, and even to commission it from time to time. This is the test of the vibrancy of a culture and its potential for renewing itself. If our role is to provide a ritual of communion that transcends political, ideological and social divisions, we obviously have to seek out and encourage new classical music that does the same. We want music that grips its audience profoundly, written by composers who understand our audience and who would be happy to be considered part of it. Sadly such composers are not easy to find. Instead it is often from the ranks of 'world music', jazz and even Early Music, that we discover things which the public do not know, but which we think they might enjoy. We try to avoid the 'ghetto-isation' of new music, which is to treat it as though it belongs outside of the mainstream of concert life or has been written for an entirely different audience. The new should be integrated into mainstream programming and should carry no stigma. That is difficult to achieve, after decades of audience alienation under the influence of dogmatic modernist orthodoxies. The damage can only be undone by treating audiences with respect and engendering a climate of trust. We have a responsibility to our audiences who are, after all, our paymasters and our foremost community.

It is our aim that the public should come with us on these varied journeys, trusting in our good judgement. If we understand who makes up our audience, and they believe in our endeavours, then our musical culture will be enlivened. If music is where the divine spark has retreated in our secular age, we must let those sparks ignite to provide a beacon. Concert halls alone cannot solve the spiritual malaise of modern times, but they can show that it is not inevitable. Enchanted spaces, animated by great music, thriving at the heart of our great cities, surely offer us hope. Perhaps our culture has not entirely forgotten that there is more to life than television and shopping.

THE ICON MAY
BECOME AN IDOL
AND VICE VERSA

SACRED MUSIC IN THEORY
Sander van Maas

I believe there is no truly profane music, nor any truly sacred music, but onereality, seen from different angles.
(Olivier Messiaen)[1]

This may seem a strange remark for a composer who regarded as his highest musical mission 'the illumination of the theological truths of the Catholic faith'.[2] Are these Catholic truths to be understood as mere *perspectives* on a (neutral, technical) musical reality? How can 'profane' and 'sacred' music ever be mediated by this reality, if the content of 'sacred' music implies a universalist and totalising view of music? Does not Messiaen here in fact reveal himself to be a sceptic with regard to the possibility of his highest mission? Unlike many of his distant predecessors, Messiaen does not seem willing to rely on a plain dichotomy between *musica sacra* and *musica profana*, or between a *prima* and *seconda prattica*. His remark reflects at one and the same time the drastic changes religious faith has undergone since the scientific revolutions of the 17th century, and his own fascination for the fruits of these very developments, which often seem to conflict with orthodox religion. He is not only known for his devout mottos and titles, but also for his ample use of pseudo-scientific methods and knowledge – even in support of the expression of his 'theological truths'. Messiaen's paradoxical combination of old and new, sacred and profane, faith and technology (combining a seemingly medieval faith with highly modernist musical technologies) may serve to illustrate the point that the ancient ideal of *musica sacra* has not simply collapsed under the pressures of secularisation processes.[3] Rather, *musica sacra* has changed its appearance and a reconsideration of its traditional tenets is called for – in particular, as I will argue, with regard to the limits of the secular – in terms that reach beyond traditional dichotomies.

Appearances to the contrary, the religious has never been absent from the Western musical tradition – not even in most recent times. As Helga de la Motte-Haber has shown in a collection of essays on *Musik und Religion*, the religious has even been of central importance to the development of musical modernism.[4] The integral re-invention of music by the

1 Antoine Goléa, *Rencontres avec Olivier Messiaen* (Paris: Slatkine, 1984), 41.

2 Olivier Messiaen, *Music and Color: Conversations with Claude Samuel* (Portland, Oregon: Amadeus Press, 1994), 20.

3 On the relation between new technologies and post-secular musical phenomena, see my 'Op wegsterven na dood', in Bart Vandenabeele and Koen Vermeir (eds.), *Gemedieerde Zintuiglijkheid* (Budel: Damon, 2003), 81-89.

4 Helga de la Motte-Haber (ed.), *Musik und Religion* (Laaber: Laaber Verlag, 1995).

Sacred music in theory

5 On Goeyvaerts' spirituality, see Reinder Pols, 'The Time is near... Karel Goeyvaerts' Apocalyptic Utopia in his Opera "Aquarius"', in Belgisch tijdschrift voor muziekwetenschap, 48 (1994), 151-172. Helga de la Motte-Haber (ed.), Geschichte der Musik im 20. Jahrhundert : 1975-2000 (Laaber: Laaber Verlag, 2000), 263.

6 More often than not, studies on this subject appear to be written by believers – believers either in the religious vision thought to be expressed by the music, or in (the) music as such. Concerning Messiaen, for instance, one finds either contributions which portray Messiaen's music as an exemplary carrier of orthodox theological meaning (the work of the French pianist-priest Jean-Rodolphe Kars is a case in point here). Or one finds musicological literature discussing Messiaen and his music in a quasi-hagiographic way, credulously reiterating the composer's every view and comment. These latter texts seem to be written from an 'amateur' and art-believer's standpoint, even though many of these authors operate in an academic context. Both types of discourse remain somewhat difficult to use in a critical debate on the possibility and nature of contemporary religious music.

7 Oskar Söhngen, Theologie der Musik (Kassel: Johannes Stauda Verlag, 1967). Albert Blackwell, The Sacred in Music (Cambridge: The Lutterworth Press, 1999).

serialists was supported by Messiaen's religious imagination, by Goeyvaerts' utopian spirituality and Stockhausen's metaphysical speculations.[5] And this involvement of the religious does seem to run deeper than it only being a superficial addition to the music 'proper'. How then do we account for the relative absence of the religious in any (systematic) discussion of these and other contemporary musics? Largely this seems to be an effect of its neglect by the reflective disciplines that address music – most importantly aesthetics, music theory and musicology. As far as the analysis of music is concerned, musicology still tends to rely on Enlightenment and formalist strategies, and often disregards the religious as an active and systematically important factor. Although musicological research often does mention the religious, it only does so as an external, thematic or historical element, reducing it, for instance, to a composer's intentions, as a programmatic narrative functioning at a merely symbolic level, or to belonging to a by and large obsolete musical-speculative heritage. Musicology – even in its counter-appearance as New Musicology – does not *address* the problem of *musica sacra* – it rather isolates and circumvents it. Instead of elucidating its transformations, it renders the notion and its affiliations even less comprehensible and leaves unanswered questions about its structure, power, meaning, use or validity in present-day musical thought, imagination and practice.

Against New Musicology

Nonetheless, contemporary critical literature on the problem of sacred music does exist.[6] Fine examples include Oskar Söhngen's *Theologie der Musik* and Albert Blackwell's recent book-length essay *The Sacred in Music*.[7]
These studies stand out as surveys of sacred music in the complex environment of present-day secularisation and of the general fading of religious structures. Through a debate with philosophy, they create a critical perspective from which both theological aesthetics and new developments such as – in Blackwell's case – New Musicology can be criticised. And this, I believe, is necessary. For despite the rise of post-structuralist and post-modern cultural and aesthetic theories, and despite their recent application to the field of music, these new musicographical currents overlook the actuality of religious (or 'religious') concepts in the composition, reproduction and consumption of music – and even in their own style of theorising.
As Blackwell has observed in his critical discussion of Susan McClary's analysis of Mozart's piano concerto in G major (K. 453), New Musicology tends to reduce any transcendentality

to the immanent categories of 'social practice'.[8] According to McClary transcendence in Mozart is an illusion wholly reducible to the musical and social practices common in the late 18th century. Listening to the concerto, she cannot but weep for the impossibility of the 'Utopia' represented.

Although I do not fully agree with Blackwell's reply to McClary (he relies too much on counter-examples and external authorities, and does not really discuss his own theological premises), I sympathise with his criticism and sense of amazement. I see no reason why a critique of the metaphysics of the theories on which McClary bases her approach, should lead to the embrace of its exact opposite, a hermetic socio-political immanentalism. How could one? – I would ask her, with the logic of deconstruction in mind. The idea of music as the result of social construction, contingent values, and negotiation (instead of as natural order, eternal value and divine givenness) still presupposes the quasi-transcendental structures of the contract, necessity and even of the absolute. For its very possibility, McClary's critical reversal of the transcendent view of music – which often is present in theological thinkers – still depends on its counterpart. It performs the sublime move of turning the world upside down, relying on its very sublimity to give her argument force. Hardly ever have I read such a solid piece of metaphysical historicism as when I read the introduction to McClary's article on Bach.[9] In my opinion, neither a simple return to a theologically informed transcendentalism, nor its rhetorical reversal can be taken as an answer to the present-day problem of sacred music. I believe a quite different discourse is required for thinking through the consequences for the study of music of the implosion of metaphysics and the 'death of God'.

These phenomena or figures of thought, which may be perceived as steps on the road to secularisation, call for a new approach to the problem of sacred music. The general fading of religion, the weakening of faith and the diminishing plausibility of a link between music and 'the religious' (whatever that may have come to signify), require an approach which both shuns a simple return to orthodox (music) theologies and a categorical farewell to the musico-theological tradition. The idea (and ideal) of sacred music may well lie in a process of fading – church bells teach us that the highest overtones sound when the sound of the bell fades away. As Gianni Vattimo writes in his book on belief, the weakening of faith means a movement towards a less simple, direct and monumental presence – a theme that is reminiscent of the history of *Kunstreligion*, of music's becoming a metaphor for religion (or 'religion'), as an ambiguous orientation towards – perhaps? – 'the secret'.[10] This weakening is exactly what brings music and religion together in the present process of fading, of diminishing – of religion's (and, in its own way, also

8 See Blackwell, *The Sacred in Music*, 105-24. SusanMcClary, 'A Musical Dialectic from the Enlightenment: Mozart's Piano Concerto in G Major, K.453', in *Cultural Critique*, 4 (Fall 1986), 129-69.

9 Susan McClary, 'The Blasphemy of talking Politics during the Bach Year', in Richard Leppert and Susan McClary (eds.), *Music and Society: The Politics of Composition, Performance and Reception* (Cambridge: Cambridge University Press, 1996), 13-62: 13-20. See also Blackwell, *The Sacred in Music*, 105.

10 Gianni Vattimo, *After Christianity* (New York: Columbia University Press, 2002).

music's) becoming less and less 'loud'. Put this way, one can hear the resonances of recent 'deconstructions of Christianity', as proposed by Derrida, Nancy and others, which analyse this very movement and take it to its extremes. With regard to the problem of sacred music in the early 21st century, I suggest to leave these resonances linger and to listen for their analytical possibilities – and to have them accompanied by the tones of various other so-called 'post-secular' philosophies.[11]

11 These issues are dealt with in more detail in my *Doorbraak en Idolatrie: Olivier Messiaen en het geloof in muziek* (Delft: Eburon, 2003), 165 ff.

12 Messiaen, *Conférence deNotre-Dame* (Paris: Leduc, 1978), 2.

The Example of Messiaen

Let me illustrate this new approach by returning to Messiaen. Messiaen has written and spoken much about his musical activities, and has done his very best to remove any ambiguities about either his intentions or his music. For a musician, one might say, this is remarkable indeed, for music does not generally seem the right medium for unambiguous statements – but that is a different subject perhaps. In a lecture from 1977, Messiaen responded to a request for clarification of his views on religious music. After paying homage to the old traditions of liturgical chant and what he confusingly calls 'religious music' (i.e. music addressing religious topics outside the liturgical context), he described a phenomenon that will guide my reflections for the remainder of this text. Placing it well above the other two levels of religious music, Messiaen introduced his personal inventions of musical 'sound-colour' (*son-couleur*) and 'dazzlement' (*éblouissement*). According to the composer, this elevated music dazzles the listener through a synaesthetic mixture of sound and colour, so powerful as to lead him or her to the experience of, in Messiaen's words, 'a breakthrough towards the beyond, towards the invisible and unspeakable'.[12]

This idea could easily be dismissed as one of those composers' dreams which should not be taken to reflect the reality of their music, if it weren't for the experience of Messiaen's music and the kinds of concepts he refers to, which do indeed call for critical reflection. For, to state that there have been times when the language of 'the sacred' was a part of everyday life, and when the idea of sacred art fitted well into general beliefs, is one thing – it is something quite different to suggest, in an apparently unmetaphorical way, in the late 20th century, that 'sacred music' can lead one to a 'beyond'. Messiaen, I should add, was not at all interested in a simple regression to obsolete models, as with John Tavener and his Orthodox musical practice. Messiaen was a part – or, more appropriately, the 'father' – of the most radical musical movement the century has seen, and incorporated the new techniques and viewpoints into his compositional style. A 'breakthrough towards the beyond' – to repeat the question –

how could this ancient (Hellenic-Christian) idea be understood at its unexpected recurrence in the contemporary (i.e. highly technological and secularised) context of music composition and appreciation? And how should it be applied to the music Messiaen left us – a music, which, as many an audience seems to agree upon, possesses a quite singular power.

The idea seems absurd, and it becomes even more so when a second lecture is taken into consideration. Many years later, in his Kyoto lecture, Messiaen repeated his claim about 'dazzlement' and 'breakthrough' and even added precise references to passages in his oratorio *La Transfiguration*.[13] What does this mean? one is led to ask. How could one imagine someone claiming to have developed the ultimate musico-mystical technique (opening a door to the beyond), daring to *localise* the concrete musical passages, suggesting that these breakthroughs are in some way produced by the musical artefact as we all know it? Would not this boil down to idolatry, blasphemy or plain arrogance? However, none of these accusations seem applicable in a simple and unambiguous way. At least, if one would like to avoid claiming the right to decide how, where and when the absolute will manifest itself. Personally, I would not dare to make such statements, and I doubt very much whether they would facilitate understanding Messiaen's singular position. For instance, it does not fit well with his claim that sacred music 'as such', in its pure or orthodox form, does not exist. In my opinion therefore, the question should rather be which *criteria* one could imagine for talking about matters relating (if that's the word) to the absolute – or somehow (more modestly) hinting at the limits of a secular, 'aesthetic' musical experience. Where, in other words, should one draw the line between aesthetics and theology, between, on the one hand, the idiom of aesthetic philosophical reflection, and, on the other hand, the language of confession, testimony (which in fact is the modality of Messiaen's statements), and revelation?

13 Messiaen, *Conférence de Kyoto* (Paris: Leduc, 1988), 14-18.

The Miracle of Aural Saturation

Obviously, this question cannot be answered simply in terms of 'here' or 'there'. Despite Messiaen's imaginary finger pointing at the score and indicating the passages of 'breakthrough', one cannot separate the domains of art and religion that easily. Turning to a more methodological analysis, one would have to assert that this is so because the languages of aesthetics and theology (or theological aesthetics, a term coined by theologian Hans Urs von Balthasar) are intimately linked - to such an extent even that a clear-cut distinction is impossible. Messiaen's project, involving the idea of a religious music, which is both religion and art (i.e. which belongs at one and the same time and equally to the domains of the absolute and that of human finitude), is but one example of 'religious art' that traverses the theoretically obscure area between philosophy and religion. In order to show the complexity of his project – i.e. his works being both 'orthodox' and 'heterodox' – I will briefly confront Messiaen's testimony with the phenomenology of French contemporary philosopher Jean-Luc Marion.[14] According to Marion, the experience of *éblouissement* (dazzlement) should be understood within a general phenomenological typology, which is oriented by 'saturation'. Technically, a 'saturated' phenomenon is distinct from its counterparts (described by Marion as the *phénomène pauvre* and the *phénomène de droit commun*) in that it shows an excess of intuition. Speaking in Husserlian terms, its 'givenness' exceeds its normative representation as an object, as constituted by the synthetic powers of the imagination and understanding.

These ideas of phenomenological excess and *éblouissement* tell us more about Messiaen's music of 'sound colours'. Exceptional though they may seem, their overwhelming and perplexing effect on the listener at once sets them apart from most other music (including most of Messiaen's other works), *and* suggests that music 'in general' may be a more complex phenomenon than formal analysis makes it appear. Relying to a great extent on the logic of the sublime, this music resists a reduction to the categories of the formal, objective and beautiful. In Marion's terms, this music resists the status of a 'poor phenomenon', and puts forward its irreducible 'excess of intuition' instead. It cannot simply be turned – by an act of analysis – into an object of knowledge, not even through its 'adequate' representation in the score, which in Messiaen's case often merely functions as a tablature. The score indicates the acts that must be performed in order to create an effect, which as such transcends the structural make-up, suggested by the musical notation. Again, this seems to be true of most music, but it has largely been neglected until the arrival of performance studies. The exceptional events in Messiaen's music leads one to believe that music in general should be interpreted as a rich and saturating phenomenon, and to acknowledge that it calls for a different kind of approach. Putting traditional methods of music analysis in brackets, one would have to look for ways to get 'beyond' or perhaps 'before' music's representation in terms of parametric and/or cognitive structures and meanings. And, as I will now argue, this alternative approach also facilitates a better understanding of Messiaen's testimony about music's *religious* potential.
One may try to leap from Marion's phenomenological, and, according to his own account, strictly philosophical, notion of saturation, to the revelatory scene evoked by Messiaen.

14 See Marion, e.g. *De Surcroît* (Paris: PUF, 2001). See for an extensive analysis of Messiaen's music of *éblouissement* my *Doorbraak en Idolatrie*.

Or, to leap from *éblouissement* and saturation, to the ominous 'percée vers l'au-delà' (breakthrough towards the beyond). For such a leap Marion relies on the double resonance of the 'givenness' philosophy presupposes in thinking the phenomenal world. Several forms of the 'saturated phenomenon' are involved in this leap. Marion's primary model for the phenomenon of 'dazzlement' is the idol, resulting from the inability of the spectator to reach beyond the seen spectacle as a mere spectacle. It is, one might say, the 'death of the gaze' or, in more auricular terms, the 'death of hearing'. One might say that to listen to Messiaen's music and to be dazzled by the aural (and also internal visual) events of saturation is to be caught in one's own inability to fully reach beyond the powers of intentionality. One touches a different dimension of musical experience (its intuitive givenness), but, in the experience of idolatry, does not fully welcome (or partly *refuses*) the effects of saturation. The musical idol is a signpost, an indication that beyond the sense structures of the musical and the musicological, 'before' the constitution of musical meaning, there might be something Other – a givenness (or *donation*) that announces itself in the idol but still waits for its revelation as a more originary characteristic of the musical phenomenon.

Marion's phenomenological typology is based partly on a distinction between the idol and the icon – the icon being the reversal of any Adornian modality of 'structural listening'. In its aural form, the icon is not experienced from the standpoint of the listener, but is rather to be understood as a 'counter-experience'. The icon is the irreducible counter-experience of givenness, in which the other reveals itself as constitutive of the subject, i.e., in the case of music, the listener. According to Marion, this reversal is the crucial moment (or *momentum*) of phenomenology and – interestingly – at the same time places the possibility of *revelation* at the heart of his 'purely' philosophical, i.e. a-theological, discipline. Givenness, belonging as it does to *both* the philosophical *and* the theological contemplation of the gift, becomes a figure in between an aesthetic of saturation and the revelation of music's having been given – inscribing both into the logic of the miracle, the arrival of the absolutely unforeseeable.[15] According to this logic, Messiaen's music of *éblouissement* and 'breakthrough' would testify to the possibility of music being a 'saturated phenomenon' – first as an idol revealing its aural excess of intuition as the splendour (*kabod, gloria*) of the sound image itself, and second, as the horizon of more intense saturation, involving a revealing reversal of aural giving in a hypothetical musical icon.[16]

15 See Marion, *Étant donné* (Paris: PUF, 1998), 185 ff.

16 This latter possibility might be identified with the ideal John Tavener hopes to realise in his compositional practice. See his remarks on this subject in John Tavener, *The Music of Silence: A Composer's Testament*, Brian Keeble, ed. (London: Faber and Faber, 1999), 107-18.

Marion's attempt to define various phenomenological types distinguished by their levels of intensity of givenness is certainly not unproblematic. As different authors have argued, the opposition between the idol and the icon can only mean that they imply each other, which rules out a clear and simple distinction: the icon may become an idol – and vice versa. But the *approach*, concentrating as it does on the quasi-theological gestures supporting the phenomenological analysis of (among others) music, may well allow analysis of seemingly absurd musico-religious statements, as in the contemporary example of Messiaen. If music is part of the phenomenology described by Marion (and according to Marion indeed it is), one may well agree to the validity of reflection on the 'absolute' character of the music of 'dazzlement', without reverting to the 19th-century discourse of absolute music and *Kunstreligion*. The problem of musical absolutism remains a vital one, as do the problems of music's 'mystical' semantic weakness, its talent for revelatory and apocalyptic gestures, and its ambiguous relationship with the sublime. All this resonates in the works of Messiaen, and in those of other composers, regardless of their private opinions about the problem of 'sacred music' (which, of course, is to be fully respected).

This brief and sketchy example may give an indication of how the analysis of music may lead to an insight into its 'theological' possibilities. These possibilities are as ambiguous as they are 'weak' – but they cannot be excluded from any aesthetic or phenomenological approach to music. Through their uncompromising resonance, their disrespectful crossing of the boundaries of music's presently preferred identity as an enlightened, autonomous and fine art, they question the limits of the secular, and show the unexpected ways in which theological and aesthetic discourses remain entangled, as, to a certain extent, they have always been. The figure of sacred music, seemingly so far removed from post-avant-garde music production that holds firmly to ideas of freedom, inventiveness, and difference, still haunts the imagination of Western music, as well as that of contemporary sound art.

At a recent exhibition in Amsterdam, a work entitled *Blue Circles* (2002) was shown by New Zealand artist Julian Dashper.[17] It consisted of a series of transparent 7-inch vinyl records, on which Dashper had recorded the sounds surrounding Jackson Pollock's *Blue Poles 11* (1952), in the museum gallery in the National Gallery of Australia where the painting is on permanent display. Initially, I found myself feeling sceptical towards these recordings of buzzing museum visitors and a very silent painting, but this scepticism disappeared once the recordings were played. How to pinpoint the staggering power one senses while listening to these

17 Seen at the exposition 'Amplified Abstraction', organised in August 2002 by Christine Sluysmans at the Art Connexion gallery in Amsterdam.

apparently nonsensical recordings? *Blue Circles* embodied the negative of Pollock's painting by recording the traces of its (possible) presence. The actual presence of the painting was rendered unimportant by the use of the 'wrong' sense. What hearing the painting uncovered was the audience's shared effort to see and to experience meaning. The listener to the recordings needs nothing but these audible traces to share this experience, and be struck by its performative power. This aspect of *Blue Circles* wonderfully describes one of the modes in which *musica sacra* is still part of present-day culture. It reminds one to listen for the inaudible, which guides the ear and fans the flame, well beyond the confines of historically established oppositions. Indeed, quoting Messiaen once more, there is no *truly* profane music, nor any *truly* sacred music – and that is why there is sacred music.

Part 3

Tradition and innovation in East and West

Dance
and
song
are
the
fundamentals
of
music

RENEWING MUSICAL TRADITION
David Matthews

In thinking about tradition, I want first briefly to consider the somewhat erratic history of music in England. In the 15th and 16th centuries, English polyphonic music was as rich as in any other part of Europe, and Tallis and Byrd are the equals of Josquin and Palestrina. In the 17th century there were a number of fine composers and one outstanding individual genius, Purcell. The 18th century was dominated by Handel: whether he counts as English I'm not sure, but if Conrad is an English novelist and curry an English food, then I think he probably can. I do feel that the melodies of *Messiah* for instance have an English character which is hard to define but easily recognizable (you find the same in Purcell). We missed out almost completely on the Classical and Romantic periods, and apart from Arne who wrote the national anthem and 'Rule Britannia', there are no English composers to speak of from Handel until Elgar, who finally was able to write the great English symphony and concerto (two of each) and also – which is not always acknowledged – the first great English string quartet. Not opera, however: this was left to Benjamin Britten, and then Michael Tippett, both of whom also wrote first-rate string quartets, and Vaughan Williams and Tippett some first-rate symphonies. It was of great advantage to 20th-century English composers that there was no national tradition of the symphony and string quartet to inhibit them, and so they were able to make substantial contributions to both of these forms.

Britten in some ways might be seen to be something of an outsider in relation to an English tradition. He began by rejecting all his English contemporaries except for his teacher Frank Bridge and, interestingly, Delius – both of whom looked more to continental models than did either Vaughan Williams or Holst. As a teenager, under the guidance of Bridge, Britten was influenced first by Debussy and Ravel and then by Schoenberg – some of his teenage music is almost atonal. This was a passing phase; in his early twenties he came under the influence of Mahler, Stravinsky, Prokofiev, Bartók and

Shostakovich, and out of all these, his earlier immersion in the music of Beethoven, and his own natural originality, he formed a very personal, firmly tonal style – perhaps the most confident use of tonality, in fact, in the mid-20th century. He made settings of poetry in French, Italian, German and Russian as well as English. All of which goes to show that eclecticism seems rooted in the English character – it can also be observed in Purcell, Elgar and Tippett. Despite Britten's interest in setting foreign languages, it is his settings of English words, in which he was influenced both by Purcell (a composer he performed and edited) and by folksongs (of which he made many settings) that most clearly define him as an English composer.

Like Elgar, Britten became a popular composer in his lifetime, largely because of his gift for melody, which seems quite unselfconscious – a rare gift in the 20th century except among popular composers like Gershwin and Irving Berlin. (The operetta *Paul Bunyan*, by the way, shows that Britten could have had a career writing Broadway musicals.) His opera *Peter Grimes* demonstrates this gift for memorable melody to a high degree and this was one of the chief reasons for its immediate success. Both Britten and Tippett took a very different approach to the characteristic modernist one of standing aloof from one's audience. This was partly from political conviction – they were both socialists (also incidentally pacifists). Both of them were insistent on the composer playing an active role in society as a communicator. Tippett's oratorio *A Child of Our Time* and Britten's *War Requiem* are both large-scale public statements on issues of war and suffering and individual conscience, written in a highly communicative musical language. Both works have affected large numbers of people while making no artistic compromises. Are such works possible nowadays in our different cultural climate? It is difficult to say a definite yes, because there seem no longer to be composers of stature who are using the kind of comprehensive musical language they did, and there also seems to be a shying away from large-scale statements by mainstream composers.

The majority of British composers since Britten and Tippett have rejected their influence, but a few have not, for instance Nicholas Maw and Judith Weir, and also myself. When I first began to compose in the 1960s it was unfashionable among my generation to compose tonally, but I was encouraged in my belief in the continuing validity of tonality by the achievement of Britten and Tippett, and I was also impressed by the way they had taken traditional forms such as the symphony and string quartet and vitally renewed them. As a composer, both these forms have been very important to me. During my lifetime I have seen a dramatic shift back to tonality by many composers, but it appears to me that all of them practise a narrower form of tonality than that used by either Britten and Tippett, which continued to employ such essential devices of classical tonality as modulation and a properly functioning bass line. I should like to quote here a passage from my essay in the book *Reviving the Muse*:

> Most contemporary tonal music is static; but stasis, it seems to me, is ideally a condition to be achieved, as for instance in Beethoven's last piano sonata where the static, contemplative slow movement is heard as a consequence of the dynamic drama of the first movement. The dynamic use of tonality will involve both modulation and the rediscovery of dissonance as a disruptive force. Although one can no longer easily define the difference between consonance and dissonance, it is still possible to conceive of harmony as either stable or unstable. Unless there are real harmonic contrasts in a piece, it cannot have dynamic movement. Perhaps, because our most frequent experience of movement nowadays is as a passenger in a car, train or plane, observing the landscape speeding by while we ourselves remain still, most fast movement in contemporary music, whether tonal or atonal, is merely rapid motion without any involvement of physical energy. Fast music in the past was related to the movement of the body, walking, running or dancing.[1]

Dance and song are the fundamentals of music. That should hardly need to be questioned, yet in the 20th century, while dance and song naturally stayed the basis of popular music, the doctrines of post-Second World War modernism tried to eliminate both dance and song from serious music and to create an irrevocable gulf between serious and popular music. This was a costly mistake. In the past, serious music had always stayed closely in touch with the vernacular language of popular and folk music, until Schoenberg renounced the use of the vernacular at the start of the last century. At first, he and a few others were very much on their own; other modernist composers such as Stravinsky and Bartók continued to base their language on folk music. Both Tippett and Britten had a creative relationship with folk music. In Tippett's early music the melodies are derived from folksong in a similar way to his predecessors Vaughan Williams and Holst; later he substituted the more contemporary vernacular of African-American blues and jazz, but the idea of a vernacular language that stood behind his music remained important for him, as it did for Britten. Britten's musical thinking was grounded in the idea of song, from his earliest childhood when his mother sang to him, and later when he accompanied her singing at the piano. Although he rejected the kind of nationalistic attitude to folksong exemplified by Vaughan Williams, Britten, as I have noted, made many highly original settings of folksongs, from Great Britain, France and the USA.

1 David Matthews, 'Renewing the Past: some personal thoughts', in Peter Davison, ed., *Reviving the Muse: Essays on Music After Modernism*, Claridge Press, London 2001, p. 205.

Classical sonata form included a dance movement, originally a minuet, then the scherzo which was at first a speeded-up minuet and then became a form in its own right. Contemporary scherzos often have little connection with dance rhythms, and it has seemed to me that composers should try to restore this lost dance element back into music. We need a contemporary archetype to replace the minuet, and it should be a popular form, known by everyone. Contemporary popular music ought to provide one, but rock music, which has abandoned the formal dance and, as Roger Scruton shows in his article, has also largely abandoned vital rhythm, may not be of much use here. But the tango seems highly suitable: its rhythms are infectious, and erotic – as both the minuet and the waltz were once considered to be, though time has now dulled them. The tango already has a historical place in European music: composers who have written tangos since the 1920s, including Stravinsky, Martinu and Schnittke; it also has its indigenous South American tradition, and there are the many tangos by Piazzola which are attempts to create a kind of folk art. But as far as I know the tango has not been used before in a symphony or a string quartet. In my Fourth Symphony I made the second of its two dance movements a tango, written in simple ternary form, and in my more recent Ninth Quartet there is a movement which contains three successive tangos, the second of which is also a development of the first, and the third a derivation from the first. This is followed by a recapitulation of all three tangos played simultaneously. So there is a connection here with sonata form, as in some of Beethoven's scherzos.

The post-war modernists, in their general renunciation of everything to do with the past, rejected the idea of repetition and development, aiming instead at a heightened sense of the moment. So that the traditional conception of a piece moving through time on a journey towards a destination was abandoned. The experiment produced some interesting results: for instance Boulez's *cummings ist der Dichter*, which is constructed rather like an artichoke where one gradually removes the leaves one by one to reveal the heart, the most precious part, within. But sonata form, which is based on the ideas of statement, development, repetition, and contrast, and which is the most sophisticated form for conveying the idea of a journey through time, seems to me to offer a far richer musical experience. Sonata form also seems an inexhaustible archetype. Like the sonnet, it is familiar to all educated people. The moment of recapitulation in a sonata movement offers a particular opportunity for innovation because of all the precedents that will subconsciously be in the minds of the audience. I can suggest here as a general principle that the more familiar a device, the more chance one has to confound expectation, which is what real innovation is. The moment of recapitulation was greatly heightened by Beethoven in his symphonies, culminating in the first movement of the Ninth Symphony where we feel a whole new world being revealed, familiar but also totally different. There is another superb example of an innovative moment of recapitulation in the first movement of Sibelius's Fifth Symphony, where the music as it were gathers itself together and finally makes a very clear statement, as if everything before had been hidden in mist and the sun has just appeared. Recapitulation cannot really operate without tonality, which is perhaps why Schoenberg more or less abandoned it in favour of continuous development. But development cannot make its full effect unless there is a return to stability.

The finale of a symphonic piece, if one is using a multi-movement form, is a problem: it has been since Beethoven's Ninth Symphony. Of Bruckner's many attempts to solve the finale problem he only succeeded absolutely once, I think, in his Eighth Symphony, and he spent the last years of his life trying in vain to complete his Ninth. We cannot now, it often seems, sum up decisively and comprehensively, perhaps because we no longer feel the confidence of composers in the past. It is probably better to end on a less serious level, as many Classical works do. I am only raising this problem to state it, not to offer solutions; but it is something that composers of the future can go on profitably addressing. I can however point here to one very successful solution to the finale problem in Britten's Third Quartet, which was almost his last work, and in which you feel that his whole life's work is at stake, if he fails to provide the right ending; but he does, and his finale is both a resolution and a new departure towards the door that he did not open.

In their string quartets, Britten and Tippett make use of old contrapuntal forms. Britten uses the chaconne form in his Second and Third Quartets, while Tippett's Second and Third Quartets contain fugues – the Third Quartet has no less than three fugal movements. The history of the fugue since Beethoven, whose fugues are the most remarkable in all music apart from Bach's, is somewhat patchy: there are few outstanding examples of later 19th-century fugues, and many are somewhat perfunctory – for example Liszt's – though there is a splendid culmination of the 19th-century conception of the fugue in the first movement of Mahler's Eighth Symphony. In the 20th century the Bachian fugue was revived by neo-classical composers, but it often sounds rather artificial and unconvincing. Tippett, on the other hand, who undertook an exhaustive study of fugue and counterpoint with a notable teacher at the Royal College of Music, R.O. Morris, took up the challenge of the dynamic, Beethovenian fugue and had remarkable success with it, especially in the Third Quartet and the finale of the First Symphony, which is modelled on the finale of the 'Hammerklavier' Sonata. Can anything more be done with this much used form? Contemporary composers would appear to think not, but I have recently turned to the fugue in my Eighth String Quartet and have also composed a series of fifteen fugues for solo violin, some of which are in four parts – Bach does not go beyond three – and which contain some formal experiments, such as a slow fugue with a fast coda, and some textural ones – a pizzicato fugue, for instance, and a tremolo one which is also palindromic.

I have come to the conclusion that there are still plenty of things to be done with this challenging form (and it is extremely challenging as one cannot help putting oneself in hopeless competition with Bach).

I have used the chaconne form myself, notably in an orchestral piece called simply *Chaconne*, which in fact consists of two chaconnes played consecutively and also in contrapuntal combination. It also has a programmatic connection with a sequence of poems by the contemporary English poet Geoffrey Hill about our first civil war, The Wars of the Roses, in particular one especially bloody battle in that war, the Battle of Towton. My piece is partly a meditation on the sombre mood of the poem sequence and partly an evocation of the battle. It consists of three consecutive sections. The first is the battle scene, which I hope illustrates my point about dissonance as a disruptive force: it is deliberately dissonant and intended to be quite shocking because it evokes painful events, but the level of dissonance here is markedly higher than in the remainder of the piece and therefore makes a more telling effect within the whole. The second section is a melody for solo viola over quiet but still dissonant harmonies; again, I think the language is appropriate here because this is intended as a lament; lastly comes a passage for strings which is an attempt to provide consolation; it's much less dissonant, and I feel that the counterpoint here is *itself* the vehicle of consolation and a more effective one than a simple harmonised melody would be. More than anything else, counterpoint enables you to raise the expressive level of your music. In fact if I had one piece of advice for a young composer it would be: learn how to use counterpoint, and I would qualify that with a remark of Busoni's: make your counterpoint melodious.

Orientalism served as an important source of musical innovation

ORIENTAL IDENTITIES IN WESTERN MUSIC
Rokus de Groot

1 Indeed, in the perspective of its relationship to the Ottomans, Europe should not be treated as a unity. While the Habsburg rulers were involved in fierce territorial conflicts with the Turks, King Francis I of France sent an ensemble of musicians to Suleyman the Magnificent in order to thank him for his support against the same Habsburgs.

Tradition and innovation in East and West

Invocation in a 'Turkish' comedy

The comedy-ballet *Le Bourgeois Gentilhomme* by Jean-Baptiste Lully contains a Turkish Ceremony, which must have caused great hilarity at the French court of Louis XIV. In this piece from 1670, which is based on Molière's play of the same title, the Ottoman Turkish episode is a comedy embedded within a comedy. The family and friends of the protagonist Mr. Jourdain bring a *muphti*, an important Muslim dignitary, into play, with the intention of having Jourdain ennobled as a high-ranking Ottoman. The latter is a *bourgeois*, but through exotic impersonations taken by those around him, he is given the illusion that he is a *gentilhomme*. By means of this playful Turkish 'conversion' they try to coerce him into giving his daughter Lucile in marriage to Cléonte, despised by Jourdain for being a fellow common citizen.

French performers and spectators greatly loved this kind of allusive play with identities, as it provided an opportunity for dressing up in exotic clothes and for having a good laugh at the funny language the foreigners on stage were using in song and speech. Thus the Turks in *Le Bourgeois Gentilhomme* speak, as a 'foreign language', a broken Italian lingo (the *muphti* is unable to conjugate verbs: 'Se ti sabir, ti respondir').

While Central Europe was involved in military and territory conflicts with Turkey, France and the Ottoman empire enjoyed an important relationship of trading. It was only a year before Lully's composition that Soliman Aga, a Turkish envoy, had visited France on a diplomatic mission. In fact, *Le Bourgeois Gentilhomme* may be seen as a theatrical 'revenge' for the behaviour of the envoy perceived by French witnesses as contemptuous.[1] It is not only Turks who are impersonated in Lully's comedy-ballet. The piece contains an elaborate *Ballet des Nations* in which representatives of some French provinces, Spaniards, and Italians figure, all of them portrayed by means of amusing habits and conversations.

There is one major difference between the ways in which the Turks and the other regional and national identities are portrayed. Before the *muphti* and his men begin their imposed comedy, they say a prayer to Allah. We hear that these Turks are impersonated by Frenchmen, as they sing major triads. At the same time, the way in which Lully sets the prayer to music shows that he had access to sources by witnesses. Allah's name is scanned in a manner very similar to how it is still done in Turkey today as in *ilahi* and *zikr*. Eleven times Lully's Turks call out to Allah, and end with 'Ekber', 'great'.

This is one example out of many European works for the theatre from the 17th century onward in which a connection is made between the world of the 'Orient' and aspects of religion and ethics. At that time of course, religion was an obvious distinctive characteristic in the definition of cultural identity. It is striking, however, that it is only the Turks among all the nations in Lully's piece who open not only their first but also their second Air with an invocation of God.

This invocation on a small scale manifests some features which are typical for the way the 'Orient' has been portrayed in Western music for centuries. Although the calling of Allah's name is fitted into the European musical idiom – sung as a major triad –, it is quite exceptional that this is done in a harmonically completely static manner: the triad is repeated without any change. Because there is no dynamic aspect in the harmonic sense, the emphasis in this passage lies on the sound and on the rhythmical aspect of music, in this case the beat.[2] In the Turkish ceremony we find a playful form of a figure more often encountered within the context of the representation of tension between religious faiths: the impersonation of Jourdain may be viewed as a temporary conversion ('mock-ennoblement').

A litany in fear of the Ottomans

For many centuries Ottoman Turkey has been the closest and also the most dreaded oriental neighbour of Europe, though this is more evident in Central and Eastern Europe than in its Western countries.[3] An echo of this may be heard in such an unlikely musical work as a church cantata of Johann Sebastian Bach. His Cantata BWV 18, *Gleichwie der Regen und Schnee vom Himmel fällt*, depicts the many perils that threaten European Christianity. There are various inner enemies, such as greed, lust and gluttony. But formidable external enemies are also active. To Bach's Lutheran copy-writer these enemies figure in two religious-geographic axes: North-South cum Lutheran-Roman Catholic, and West-East cum European Christian-Ottoman Muslim. In the second *recitativo* of the Cantata, the soprano implores God:

2 See P. Gradenwitz, *Zwischen Orient und Okzident. Eine Kulturgeschichte der Wechselbeziehungen*, Wilhelmshaven/Hamburg, Heinrichshofen 1977 for a Western music history of derivation from, and representation of non-Western musical practices and structures. The terms 'harmony' and 'harmonic' refer to Western traditions of tonality.

3 The Ottoman empire lasted from 1299-1923, while it was at the summit of its power in the 16th and 17th centuries.

Und uns für des Türken und des Pabsts grausamen Mord und Lästerungen, Wüten und Toben väterlich behüten. ('And fatherly protect us from the horrible murder and defamation, raging and raving of the Turk and the Pope').

In this early cantata Bach employs an exceptional musical way of text setting, the litany. The soprano sings her intense prayer to God on a single tone as in heightened speech. It The monotony and rhythmic ostinato of the musical litany setting are striking, and invite comparison with Lully's *ilahi*.
The Central-European fear for the Turks was still quite alive in Bach's days. It was only two years before the year of his birth, 1685, that the Ottoman siege of Vienna had been dismantled. It had been a long ordeal, from its imposition in 1529 by Suleyman the Magnificent.

A stile concitato clash between two faiths

A high degree of rhythmic ostinato and monotony have been used in another, much earlier reflection of the religious-geographic tension between the Christian West and the Islamic East, in Monteverdi's *Combattimento di Tancredi e Clorinda*. This composition in the *genere rappresentativo*, first performed in 1624, and published in 1638 as part of the *Madrigali Guerrieri ed Amorosi*, deals with the fierce combat between the Crusader Tancredi and the valiant Muslim knight Clorinda. The oriental lady has disguised herself as a male fighter; Tancredi does not know the true identity of his adversary with whom he is actually in love. A long and terrifying battle gives Monteverdi ample opportunity to test his new *stile concitato*. This music of ostinato experiments provides the sound of a clash between two competing faiths.
Finally Clorinda receives a mortal wound. It is at this moment that a common theme within the context of inter-religious combat and love between Christians and Muslims appears in the *Combattimento* – and in Tasso's *Gerusalemme Liberata*, which provided the text: conversion. It is Clorinda's last wish to be baptized, a wish which is granted. This step appears to be not too great: earlier in *Gerusalemme Liberata* it is related that Clorinda had received a Christian upbringing as a child. Maybe the gulf between Muslim and Christian was too wide for Tasso to bridge by a straightforward conversion.[4]
Though Torquato Tasso's text *Gerusalemme Liberata*, first published 1581, refers to the First Crusade of 1096-1099, when the Ottoman Empire had not yet come into being, the composition of that epos does relate to the contemporary tense relationship between the Ottoman and European powers. While the former were threatening Central Europe and were rivals in the Mediterranean, calls for a new crusade were heard in Europe.

4 There are also many stories in Islamic traditions of reverse conversions. One of the most famous is the one about sheikh Sa'nan, told by the 13th-century Sufi Fariduddin Attar from Nishapur in his *Mantiq-ut-Tayr* (The Conversation of the Birds). The sheikh had the ill luck of falling in love with a mischievous Byzantine lady, who at some point went so far as to demand of him that he herd her pigs as a token of his love. Finally he comes to his senses, and leaves her. In a dream the lady gets the message that she has lost the chance of receiving the true faith. She travels after sheikh Sa'nan who converts her.

The memory of the 1571 epic sea battle of Lepanto was still fresh, at which the Ottoman fleet was beaten by a 'Holy League' of Southern European states.

'Turkish' sonorous violence and the grace of a renegade

In our assessment of East-West relationships in European theatrical arts, Mozart's *Entführung aus dem Serail* ('Abduction from the Seraglio', 1781/82) should not be absent. The construction of an Ottoman 'Turkish' Orient is clearly audible, and it is again the sound aspect – here explicitly in the sense of timbre – which is responsible. We witness the late 18th century fashion of representing the military music of the Janissaries, the elite military corps of the Ottoman Empire (originally *yeniçeri*, 'new troops'). Right from the start, in the overture, Mozart presents us with a very effective musical staging of the fear for the Ottoman Turks. The strings open the work softly – nobody senses any danger –, then suddenly a 'Turkish' sonorous violence takes the public unawares. After some time a sensitive 'European' kind of music, in a minor key refined with incidental chromatic details, replaces the din, but it is not long before the Janissary major key music bursts forth again for a relentless sonorous beating of the listeners.[5] Harmonically the music of the Janissaries is embedded in European tonality, but in the field of timbre it is non-European. Mozart uses instruments, which can count as 'Turkish': the *tamburo turco*, cymbals, triangle and *flauto piccolo*.

In a European context it is striking that the former two instruments lack discrete pitch – the very foundation of harmonic tonality. Therefore they explicitly constitute a *corpus alienum* in the 18th century orchestra. This orchestra did include percussion instruments, the kettledrums, but they are tuned.[6] The absence of discrete pitch may be taken as a token of 'barbarity'. Precisely this absence emphasizes the rhythmic and timbre role of these instruments. (In fact, Berlioz would later call the Janissary tradition within European orchestras 'the colouring of rhythm'.[7]) In this sense, an 'oriental' identity manifests itself in the overture of *Die Entführung*, in a way which is comparable to some extent to the Turkish Ceremony in Lully's *Le Bourgeois Gentilhomme*; in both cases the 'Orient' is connected with a percussive quality without tonal differentiation.

Again the world of the 'Turkish-oriental' is linked with matters of religion. A Spanish company has run ashore on an Ottoman coast. The lady among them, Konstanze, has fallen into the hands of the Bassa (pasha) Selim. His servant Osmin guards her. A stratagem conceived of by Belmonte, Konstanze's lover, and Pedrillo, for liberating the lady in distress, fails, and the whole European party is captured. They fear for their lives.

5 We may hear an echo of the Janissary music in present-day Turkish *mehter* (military) music. Sultan Mahmud II abolished the Janissaries corps, in 1827, however, by murdering its members. The Turkish musicologist Emre Araci is preparing a book on Giuseppe Donizetti, the brother of Gaetano, who revived the military music corps for the sultan.

6 See Roger Scruton's reference to the fact that in Western popular music of the 20th century the rhythmic aspect has been 'externalized' and transferred to percussion instruments without discrete pitch. In that sense this music has distanced itself from the Western classical-romantic tradition, in which rhythm, together with melody and harmony builds an integrated whole. As is clear from the present example already instances of rhythmic externalization can be found from the last quarter of the 18th century, in connection with the European construction of 'oriental' identity. See also Berlioz's qualification of the Janissary convention within the European symphony orchestra as 'colouring of rhythm' (in the present text).

7 See H.G. Farmer, *Military Music*, London: Parrish 1950, p. 37.

The 'Turk' after all is stereotypically known to be despotic and to show no mercy to foreigners. This fear only increases when it becomes apparent that Bassa Selim has at one time been wronged by Belmonte's father and therefore has a very good motive for revenge. The Viennese public certainly must have expected Bassa Selim to act brutally, and satisfy the cliché of 'oriental' cruelty.

Indeed, in *Die Entführung* we encounter all the European stereotypes of the Ottoman Turk. Especially Osmin is an epitome of 'Turkish identity': he is stupid, lustful and cruel. No one who has heard it will ever forget the stubborn insistence of this man that he, too, has got brains ('Ich hab' auch Verstand'). The Turkish protagonist Bassa Selim turns out to be a man of utter refinement, nobility and ethic maturity, however. In fact, his reaction to the fact that he holds Belmonte, the son of his Roman-Catholic Spanish enemy, turns him into an emblem of Christian virtue. It sets him apart from the other protagonists, both Turkish (Osmin) and mistrusting Christian ones (and probably also from his Spanish adversary, Belmonte's father, about whom the play does not give much information). Bassa Selim does *not* retaliate the suffering inflicted upon him by Christians, as he refrains from causing similar pain to his Spanish prisoners. Although he has fallen in love with Konstanze, he sets all Christians free with his blessings.

   This portrayal in Mozart's opera of a Turkish ruler as a man of virtue may be conceived as a reflection of a change in attitude towards the Orient, and in particular towards the world of Islam in late 18th century Europe. In the wake of the Rational Enlightenment, attempts to integrate Islamic history into universal history replace the earlier inimical preoccupation with Islam. Translations of the *quran* still appear accompanied with the usual derogatory commentary of it being a falsification of the Bible. A late example of this can be found in David Friedrich Megerlin's 1772 German translation; it contains a portrait with the caption 'Mahomed, the false prophet'.[8] One of the first influential writers to bring change to the appreciation of the world of Islam is Johann Jacob Reiske (1716 – 1774), who laid the foundations of Arabic studies as a discipline in Germany. Another scholar whose work contributed to the flourishing of this tradition was Joseph von Hammer-Purgstall (1774-1856), a great translator of Arabic, Persian and Turkish poetry. His Hafiz translation was to inspire Goethe to write his *Der West-östliche Divan* (created in 1814/15). New stereotypes of oriental man emerge, especially through Persian poetry: refinement, sensuality, magnanimity, and clemency now prevail. As Annemarie Schimmel puts it, 'The Orient was now regarded no longer only as the home of the Anti-Christ but also as a fairyland filled with wonders (...)'.[9]

8 At a later date Goethe heavily criticized Megerlin, calling for a poetic translation of the *quran*. This task was accomplished by Friedrich Rückert, many decades after Goethe's death however.

9 A. Schimmel, *Islam, An Introduction*, New York: State University of New York Press 1992, p. 4; see also the Introduction of her book, from which the information for this passage has been derived.

Although in *Die Entführung* a shift in the European perception of the 'Ottoman Turk' is noticeable, from cruelty to nobility of soul, and from a response of fear to one of sympathy, some reserve can still be felt. Again a connection is made between the Orient and religion, in a surprising way. It would probably have been too much for Mozart's contemporaries for an oriental as Bassa Selim to be ethically superior, and an example of the Christian virtue of declining to requite the wrongs visited upon one. It is quite likely therefore that, in Scene 4, Act 1, the tension between two religious-geographical areas was lessened by the librettist, when he put the following words into the mouth of Pedrillo, as he addresses Belmonte who fears for Konstanze's honour and life:

10 Note that Clorinda also was 'really' a Christian by education.

> She has not fallen into the worst hands, *The Bassa is a renegade*, and he has retained so much delicacy that he does not coerce any of his wives to have love with him. (Translation and italics RdG)

The conversion theme reappears. The great Turk seems to be a Muslim, but 'originally' he was a Christian. The deafening 'oriental' sound of Islam – the Janissary music of the overture – turns out to be essentially alien to the identity of this refined '"Turkish"' (double quotation marks) nobleman.[10]

As in the case of Lully, efforts have been made in *Die Entführung*, to present musical articulations of a 'Turkish' identity. In these examples the representations of the 'Orient' still remain alien, both dramatically and in sound: an unusual religious worship as a comedy within a comedy, and the guise of a brutal sound-world connected with the world of a renegade respectively.

Indeed, these orientalisms do not seem to alter the foundation of the dominant musical system. Thus the *muphti* and his men perform their call to prayer in *Le Bourgeois Gentilhomme* in major triads. And in *Die Entführung*, the music of the Janissaries largely remains within the Western harmonic tonality of the time, though some percussion sounds transgress ('retrogress') it.

However, the musical portrayal of oriental identity in Mozart's work did anticipate a remarkable metamorphosis of the *sound* of Western music. In the context of musical orientalism, many additions to the Western orchestra were to come, having been imported from non-Western traditions, especially in the field of percussion. The new aspects of sound, connected with harmonic immobility, rhythmic repetitiveness and non-pitch percussion, which were all untypical in the European context, would become the hallmarks of 'oriental' identity in the Western classical music tradition. In line with the more recent late 18th century inclusion of oriental stereotypes as sensuality and refined behaviour, the musical representations are not limited to percussive qualities, but extend to timbre differentiation. 'Oriental' sound reflections became increasingly important in Western classical music until, in some works of Debussy and Stravinsky, they became dominant, often in fact with relation to the 'Orient' or to pre-Christian antiquity, as both refined and 'barbarous'. Orientalism in music, more in particular representations of conflict between a cultural 'self' and 'other', thus served as an important source of musical innovation in Europe. In some sense, a process of sonorous 'conversion' in Western music was unfolding.

Two Indian missionaries of sound

A significant contribution to the Western concept of the strong relationship between the Orient, musical sound and religion was effected by travels to the West at the turn of the 19th and 20th centuries by a number of highly gifted and multi-faceted personalities from India. When this took place, these men were colonized subjects of Great Britain, at a time when aspirations of independence were developing in India, or at least some recognition of the value of Indian traditions for their own sake was growing. The oriental travellers explicitly conceived of themselves as missionaries dedicated to transforming humanity. They thought the time had come for such a mission. The travellers experienced the destructive sides of Western secular modernity in their own environment, and pointed especially to its preoccupation with materiality, while on the other hand they conceived of India as essentially a haven of spirituality. Their ideal was to combine the material and spiritual qualities of the two, thus uniting humanity. The fact that their mission originated from colonized territory gave it poignancy. They did not only appeal to be considered as equals with Westerners, but also as healers of the world.

It so happened that two of the most influential of them, Hazrat Inayat Khan and Rabindranath Tagore were also excellent musicians, composers and singers. In the context of East-West relationships, this again implies the concept of conversion through sound.

As an Indian Sufi, Hazrat Inayat Khan (1882-1927), was initiated into traditions in which sound, and in particular music, can serve as a medium for gaining and maintaining physical and psychological balance, and ultimately, as a privileged means of attaining awareness of God, and enlightenment. The essence of Sufism has been formulated as 'direct knowledge and personal religious experience of God's presence', reached 'by means of a series of stages and states'.[11] Inayat Khan saw music, more than any other art or practice, as divine. To him it was not so much its syntactical dimension, which was important but rather its sonorous aspect: vibration. The omnipresent origin of creation is, in his conviction,

11 See G. Farrell, *Indian music and the West*, Oxford: Clarendon 1997, p. 147-155. The quotation is from p. 148, and refers to J.L. Esposito, *Islam: The Straight Path*, Oxford: Oxford University Press 1991.

'soundless', 'non-struck' sound, which may manifest itself in subtle vibrations and which may condense into physical sound, sounding music, matter and living organisms. He maintained that every form of beauty in nature, in the arts and in character is essentially soundless music. What makes music a privileged spiritual road, according to Inayat Khan, is, that man may become aware of God, the very Formless, through this medium, since he holds music free from form or thought. To him, other arts are tied to thought and form, and therefore easily conduce towards idolatry.[12] In this we hear at one and the same time his Muslim and Hindu backgrounds, his rejection and consequently extraordinary sensitivity to idolatry, as well as the concept of *Nada Brahma* – sound as creative principle. Through this spiritual foundation of music, Inayat Khan also recognized music as a universal language. At least initially, he used music as a prominent vehicle for his mission to the West.[13] Inayat Khan set himself the task of bringing the West into tune with the sonorous origin of creation.

Tagore (1861-1941) too, in his writings and lectures, which received massive attention in the West on both sides of the ocean during the Interbellum, presented music as the preferred medium for becoming aware of the divine in creation – including in one's own existence. Among the different strands in the fabric of Tagore's background were the Vaishnavite and Baul traditions of Bengaul. In both these traditions, the sensuousness and sensuality of creation are highly valued. The adjective Vaishnavite comes from Vishnu, which in the Hindu tradition is seen as the aspect of the divine, which sustains the creation, e.g. as it is enjoyed by one of his incarnations, Krishna and his devotees. Thus both in Inayat Khan's and in Tagore's public appearances and writings, the sonorous rather than the syntactical aspects of music were emphasized as a door to spiritual perception.

The context in which these Indian travellers were seen, both in their own eyes and in the eyes of their audiences, was not so much a difference of religion, as was the case in Lully's and Mozart's time, but rather a polarity between secularity and spirituality. Especially in the second half of the 19th century many movements of religious and spiritual revival arose in the West as an antidote to secular modernity, referring to Christian as well as oriental religious traditions. These movements made Western audiences receptive to the message of the Indian spiritual travellers.

It was through them, that the Western image of the Orient became connected, even more strongly than before, with spirituality, through the sonorous aspect of music. Thus when Ravi Shankar, travelled as a sitar player in the West from the late fifties onwards, he was struck by the fact that he was greeted as a mediator of meditation – and he used this well in his own performances. Also in India itself a process of the

12 Inayat Khan, *Muziek en mystiek. Soefisme en de harmonie der sferen*, Katwijk: Panta Rhei, 1991.

13 Inayat Khan did not conceive the application of music as a mechanistic affair. Not all sound and not all music would do as a way to sensing divine presence. It required a master to detect what sound would be suitable for a person at a particular time, to mature spiritually.

spiritualization of music had been going on, especially since Independence (1947).[14] It is significant in this context that when the Beatles embraced Indian music for a time, this was full of spiritual undertones and overtones, as they and their audience endeavoured 'to expand consciousness'. The sound of the *sitar* served as an emblem for such expansion.

The basic features of the connection between the East, religion and the emphasis on the sound aspect of music were already noticeable in European music of the 17th and 18th centuries, as has been indicated above in the examples from Lully and Mozart. But there is a difference in reception compared with the late 19th and 20th centuries. While in the former cases the emphasis lies on the strangeness of 'Eastern' sound and religion, in the latter instances efforts are made to appropriate possibilities of spiritual development through music. Tagore's poems, such as from his Noble prize winning collection *Gitanjali*, with their omnipresent reference to music as a spiritual road, have been widely set to music by Western composers. From the 1950s onwards his own melodies have also been reworked and harmonized by Westerners. This has been done in a quite serious way, without any trace of caricature or comedy.[15] Already in the mid-1940s, but especially in the course of the 1960s, Westerners have been engaged in the performance of Indian classical dance and music, in an anti-materialistic, spiritualistic vein. The hippie-movement led many Western youngsters to India, where they were after changes in thinking, speaking, dress and making music, strongly resembling a conversion.

A number of factors in the cultural traditions of the West around 1900 helped as well as hampered the reception of Inayat Khan and Tagore. A favourable condition was that the sonorous aspect of music had gained ever more attention from composers, performers and listeners during the 19th century. This was partly due to the very practice of representing oriental identities in music through articulations of timbre to which Mozart had already contributed. But equally important was the privileged position of classical music among the arts. Great spiritual depth was ascribed to music by philosophers like Schopenhauer, as the art through which the World Soul could sound more directly than through other human media. It is not difficult to find in Inayat Khan's and Tagore's works statements about music which show a striking similarity to those by 19th-century Western poets and philosophers, who created the ideology of classical music as the art towards the condition of which all other arts strive.[16] The latter and the Sufi Inayat Khan have in common that they build upon traditions related to the concept of the 'harmony of the spheres'. Both also share an emphasis on the 'imagelessness' of music.

There is also a considerable gulf between the Indian missionaries of sound, and most of the participants in

14 This was one of the themes of the International Conference *Music and the Art of Seduction*, organised by the Department of Musicology of the University of Amsterdam and the Society for Ethnomusicology 'Arnold Bake', Amsterdam, May 2005.

15 For an overview of the situation in the Netherlands, see R. de Groot, 'Van Eeden en Tagore. Ethiek en muziek', in *Tijdschrift van de Koninklijke Vereniging voor Nederlandse Muziekgeschiedenis* 49/2, 1999, p. 98-147.

16 See Walter Pater's dictum "All art constantly aspires towards the condition of music" (W. Pater, *The Renaissance*, Londen: Macmillan 1900: 135).

Western classical music practices, however. In contrast to the latter, Inayat Khan and Tagore never considered music to be an autonomous or absolute art. They did not consider subscribing to aestheticism. To them, music as a 'divine' art was fundamentally heteronomous, and ultimately a spiritual exercise. It is significant that at the end of his life Inayat Khan gave up musical practice, as a sacrifice. As he wrote, it was time for him no longer to play an instrument, rather to serve *as* an instrument of his creator.

Western composers as devisers of spiritual exercises through music

After the Second World War, it was Western composers who reinvigorated the bond between the Orient, sound and spirituality. This time references to oriental sources were factors, which deeply changed the concepts of the musical work, of the author, of the listener, and of the performance. In some cases the polarity deepened between Western secularism, related to aestheticism, and the concept of absolute music on the one hand, and spirituality through music, related to oriental sources, on the other.[17] Composers as Ton de Leeuw (1926-1996) and John Tavener (born 1944) formulated musical poetics tending towards spiritual orientalism. The connection between the East, sound and spirituality, which had already existed in the West, now appeared in the form of the concept of 'music as a spiritual exercise' developed by Western composers. Sometimes the fact that a musical composition is a work of art is conceived as secondary, or even as irrelevant. Some even abandon the concert hall. For Cage any environment is fit for the experience of music (or of sound, since the term music has become less appropriate) in principle. Tavener removes the performance to venues, which traditionally are seen as sacred, such as cathedrals. In Cage's work attention to music as sound rather than as syntactical structure became radicalized, partly through his contact with Eastern sources.

The socio-political situation had changed since the days of Inayat Khan and Tagore. In a first phase of post-colonialism, one encounters a spirit of discovery of oriental sources, not as preceding or subordinate to Western traditions, but as alternative or even superior ones.[18]

Concluding remarks

For centuries 'oriental' musical identities have been articulated in Western music. What is common to them is their connection with religion or spirituality, and their emphasis on sonorous rather than syntactical aspects of music, sometimes

17 Quite frequently it is neglected that both the concept and practice of absolute music are strongly determined by metaphysics. See, however, J. Christiaens, *'Kunstreligion' en het Absolute in de Muziek*, Leuven: Katholieke Universiteit Leuven 2003. About the various positions hinted at in this parapraph, see J. Cage, *Silence*, Middletown, Conn.: Wesleyan University Press 1961; J. Harvey, *In Quest of Spirit. Thoughts on Music*, Berkeley etc.: University of California Press 1999; T. de Leeuw, 'Back to the Source' in *Ton de Leeuw*, ed. J. Sligter, transl. J. Lydon, Luxembourg: Harwood 1995, p. 73-93 (originally 1992); T. Takemitsu, *Confronting Silence*, Berkeley: Fallen Leaf Press 1995; J. Tavener, *The Music of Silence. A Composer's Testament*, ed. B. Keeble, London/New York: Faber & Faber 1999; R. de Groot, 'Jonathan Harvey's Quest of Spirit through music' in *Organised Sound* 5/2 (2000), p. 103-109.

18 In the present article 'music' generally refers to Western classical and avant-garde practices; popular music practices deserve discussion in their own right.

stressing rhythmic ostinato and harmonic immobility as well. Orientalism in music, more in particular representations of conflict or fascination with a cultural 'other', served as an important source of musical innovation.

From the 16th through 18th centuries these articulations were often related to geo-political and religious tensions between Europe and the Ottoman world. Musically, one finds instances of an emphasis on rhythmic ostinato and timbre aspects, combined with harmonic stasis. Imitation of the music of the Ottoman Janissaries features a markedly percussive aspect, a symptom of military strife. In this context instruments without discrete pitch were introduced in the Western symphony orchestra, like cymbals and the 'Turkish' drum. As such these instruments figure as *corpora aliena* in the orchestra, which was tuned to the fundamental concepts of harmonic tonality. Probably this 'externalization' of the rhythmic aspect of music was conceived as an embodiment in sound of 'barbarity'.

At the end of the 18th century a change in attitude towards the world of Islam set in, generally speaking becoming more favourable, adding new stereotypes of 'oriental' man to existing ones like cruelty, despotism and stupidity, in particular, refinement, nobility, magnanimity, clemency, as well as sensuality. This brings with it an extension of musical 'oriental' reflections in the shape of an ever-greater differentiation within the realm of sound. 'Orientalism' was one of the factors which profoundly changed the sound of the Western symphony orchestra during the later 19th and early 20th centuries, however much later scholars may have belittled this change as 'superficial'. In a sense, the orchestra underwent a sound 'conversion'. Extension of percussion without discrete pitch, harmonic immobility and timbre finesse were the hallmarks of this orientalism.

A recurring theme in connection with Western musical articulations of oriental identities well into the 20th century is conversion, a concept geared to lessen the tension caused by the competition between religions (e.g. Christian and Muslim) to the spectators and listeners involved. This may occur playfully, as in the travesty of a Turkish Ceremony in Lully's *Le Bourgeois Gentilhomme*. Or it may be implied or hinted at by more or less oblique references, as in Monteverdi's *Combattimento di Tancredi e Clorinda*, or in Mozart's *Entführung aus dem Serail*. In both cases the Muslim protagonist is 'really' a Christian.

Indian missionaries of sound such as Hazrat Inayat Khan and Rabindranath Tagore strongly confirm the European topical connection between the East, music (or sound in general) and religiosity/spirituality. This 'oriental' musical identity is typically heteronomous and thus provides a contrast to the Western concept of absolute music. At the same time these oriental missionaries could relate to their Western publics through the privileged position of absolute music among the arts in Europe. Again the theme of conversion is present, in this case conversion from materialist secular modernity to spirituality. Inayat Khan and Tagore came with the intention to heal humanity, by bringing East and West into harmony, in which music was intended to play a key role. And again it is the sonorous rather than the syntactical aspects of music, which they considered relevant.

While Islam had been considered in Europe for a long time as a rival religion, European philosophers and artists were generally more receptive to religious and spiritual traditions from South-East and East-Asia introduced as fields of scholarly study since the late 18th century in Europe (Hinduism, Buddhism). After World War II it was Western composers themselves who took up strongly the relation between the Orient, (musical) sound and religion/spirituality. Their endeavours are far removed from the 'oriental' comedy within a comedy of a Lully. They apply Eastern musical and spiritual sources in devising music as a spiritual exercise. This is especially the case since the late 1960s, when e.g. Stockhausen presented music as an instrument of spiritual illumination, referring to Vedic and Yogic practices. It is certainly not rare to once again hear statements of conversion in relation to music, fundamentally conceived as a heteronomous medium of revelation. With composers like Tavener this coincides with a strong anti-modernist attitude.

Composers such as Jonathan Harvey try to justify the privileged role of music as a spiritual medium by means of oriental (Buddhist) sources. Again it is the sonorous aspect of music, which is central here, in this case composition through spectrality. Because of the unpredictability of spectral configurations, Harvey conceives music as being able to transport the listener beyond linear time, thus becoming parallel – and even *near*-identical – with spiritual experiences. Oriental musical identity, characterized by heteronomy, emphasis on the domain of sound, as well as religious and spiritual interpretation, has become part of Western new music. Also the work of Asian composers, like Takemitsu and Yun, who have entered the realm of avant-garde music, complies with this conception.

In speaking of the connection in the West between concepts of the Orient, sound and spirituality, we have travelled from a comedy within a comedy to the serious business of a spiritual search for illumination. We find a recent tendency among Western composers towards anti-aestheticism and a new functionalism of music, even to the extent of no longer making 'religious music', but making music as a religious exercise. One of the factors in this process may have been the urge composers felt to combat a sense of irrelevance of the new music intended for the classical and the avant-garde stage – by devising music

which is presented as crucial for maturation.[19]
Present-day practices of music and religion/spirituality
arouse a host of questions. What 'oriental' musical identities
are developing right now given the present-day dynamism of
globalization, with its new conventionality of stereotyping?
Is the reference to oriental spiritual sources first and foremost
a composer's instrument for musical innovation or a way of
spiritual maturation? Or to put it more simply: does ('oriental')
religion/spirituality serve music in the first place, or the other
way round? How to assess and criticize the ways composers
interpret oriental spiritual sources? What will be the difference,
if the primary concern of the composer is either musical
invention, or spiritual speculation?

These questions also bear upon cultural politics. Is it at all
possible to formulate a policy of financial support for musico-
spiritual practices? Expertise has been developed to assess
musical innovation, but what about the assessment of spiritual
maturation? Is the audience called to develop other styles of
listening, which would entail initiation into the composer's
('oriental') spiritual worlds, or can the public continue to
draw upon ways of listening within an aesthetic perspective?
How to reconcile composers' references to oriental mystical
sources, which often emphasize the figure of silence, with the
usual present-day requirement of (and eagerness for) public
exposure? What are the present-day needs and possibilities of
'hidden' musico-spiritual practices even when practiced in the
public domain?
If the distinction between 'spiritual' and 'musical' is artificial
here, do these notions completely coincide, and if not, where
do they differ, and how do such differences bear upon ways
of listening? What is happening to the concept and role of
music when listeners are viewing music as absorbing and even
replacing religious and spiritual practices?

19 Klaas de Vries raised
the matter of a sense
of irrelevance of their
artistic work being
experienced by new
music composers,
during the conference
'Redefining Musical
Identities in the 21st
Century' mentioned in
the Introduction.

Tradition and innovation in East and West

The
bad
times
lasted
too
long

MUSIC FROM THE OUTSKIRTS OF EUROPE: THE CASE OF SERBIA
Borislav Cicovacki

1 Milan Kundera,
Testaments Betrayed,
London & Boston
1996, p 192.

> Small nations haven't the comfortable sense of being there
> always, past and future; they have all, at some point or another
> in their history, passed through the antechamber of death:
> always faced with the arrogant ignorance of the large nations,
> they see their existence perpetually threatened or called into
> question ...[1]

Not every part of our little continent possessed, during the
latter portion of the history of Western civilization, such
historical-sociological conditions which could hold it tied to
the knot of cultural events which formed the pith of European
art in the 20th century. The Balkan Peninsula was an area
through which non-European influences penetrated into our
continent almost continually and in the easiest and most direct
way, remaining longest on the Peninsula itself. Let us only
remember that the greatness, permanence and universality
of Ancient Greek art result from its outstanding capacity of
selecting from extra-European ideas. And this is precisely
the art that lies at the foundation of European culture. Such
a position was secured additionally by its extended impact
through Byzantine art, which largely influenced medieval
painting, but also through Russian music (church chants and
neumatic notation).

However, the natural geographical link between the Balkans
and Asia Minor also caused the severe and until this day
unredressed consequences of the forcible interruption of the
development of European culture on the Peninsula. After the
end of the 14th century when Balkan states ceased to exist, the
history of the Peninsula can be divided into two: Turkish rule
(four and a half centuries), and a period of relative freedom,
filled with frequent wars (a century and a half).

As far as Serbian music is concerned (whose tradition is
reduced exclusively to folk and church music) this literally
means that the experiences of European music were beginning
to be transferred only at the beginning of the 20th century.
This transfer of experience was quite rapid. It was carried

out by the first Serbian composers, educated in Western Europe and Prague: composers who were aware that musical baroque, classicism and a great part of romanticism remained totally obscured in their country. The musical language of these composers is related to late romanticism, and their contribution to drawing European music closer to Serbia has been invaluable. Thus, it is owing to them that the first Serbian opera was created in 1902, and the first symphony in 1907. Performing practice in Serbia underwent major changes only after World War I however: the Belgrade Opera was established in 1920, the Belgrade Philharmonic Orchestra in 1923, and the Music Academy in 1937. Among the major composers of that period, it was perhaps Petar Konjovic who took things furthest, mostly in his operas, which were directly influenced by the operas of Leos Janácek. However, the young Serbian composers of the first half of the 20th century felt a strong need for close contacts with Europe, and this was the essential factor which brought about the rapid development of Serbian music. From the first, somewhat Bruckner-like, symphony to the first atonal composition took a mere 23 years!

The first composer whose creative period coincided with the streams of European music, and with the Bartókian treatment of folk tradition was Josip Slavenski (1896-1955). As a pupil of Kodály and Bartók, he abandoned the usual practice of romantic and exotic approaches to musical folklore, addressing instead its harmonic-melodic essence, which served as the foundation for his copious creative output. His specific contribution to that particular stream of 20th-century music lies in the use of the so-called ancient Slavic five-tone scale (a-c-d-e-g), and in original orchestration based on the laws of acoustics, especially on the disposition of harmonics, whereby he achieved unusual sonic combinations. Between the two world wars, Slavenski was highly esteemed, his works frequently performed in Europe, and he was the first Yugoslav composer whose work was published by a foreign publisher (Schott).

The importance of Slavenski to Serbian music does not end there. Apart from being an early forerunner of the utterly particular attitude of Serbian composers towards their musical heritage (the style which would actually arise in the mid-50s), he also played an important part in educating and directing young composers. He sent several of his Belgrade students for further schooling to Prague, which in the 30s of the previous century was one of the most renowned centres of the European musical avant-garde. These young composers adopted atonality, a-thematicism, and even Haba's microtonality as elements of their expressionism, and their work earned great recognition at international festivals. The most important among them – Ljubica Maric – was to become a creator who would stamp Serbian music with the most original and momentous mark precisely in the 50s. However, in the 30s, she and several of her colleagues represented the first young generation of Serbian composers who could freely write in accordance with the achievements of the European avant-garde of the time.

Two brutal historical events thwarted the European-integrative tendency of Serbian music: World War II and the triumph of communist ideology in Yugoslavia. The latter event once again blocked the exchange of information, and brought about the separation of Serbian music from Western European trends. The first and foremost blow was struck by socialist realism, a propaganda aesthetics formed in the 30s in the Soviet Union, which after World War II was forced upon the newly-formed socialist states. Social realism in music meant a ban on all elements of the inter-war avant-garde, and it dictated a return to the simple, stylized folk song, which generally assumed the form of choral mass songs on revolutionary themes. All composers of the Serbia of these days succumbed to the decrees of the Communist Party, adapting to them either by retreating into innocent romanticism, or by exploring folk music, or simply by ceasing to compose.

A slackening of this disastrous aesthetics of socialist realism took place in the mid-50s, and this induced Serbian composers to search for new possibilities which would satisfy their own urge to compose, without risking overtly going against the general role of art in socialism however. These possibilities relied primarily on the two directions of pre-war European music: neoclassicism, and expressionism with dodecaphonic elements. However, in a majority of composers these two directions somehow became anachronistically transformed, producing a kind of hybrid with romanticism (the absence of which in the history of Serbian music is felt to this day); this fact accounts for many expressionless and nonsensical compositions. It was then, however, during the 50s, that the oeuvre of two composers dramatically changed the general direction of Serbian music, giving it its authentic shape. It was mainly the achievement of Ljubica Maric, who without a doubt is Serbia's greatest composer.

Brought up in the spirit of the Serbian musical tradition, educated at the well-springs of the inter-war European avant-garde, Ljubica Maric (1909) in her mature creative period managed to fuse these two contradictory types of musical thinking in a singularly masterful and original way. In her first master piece, the cantata *Songs of Space (Pesme prostora)*, she goes beyond Bartók, reaching the primordial essence of Balkan musical language, and weaving it into a dense musical texture of expressive colours, liberated from all harmonic and melodic conventions. That is why the premiere of this work in December 1956 is considered the single most important event in the post-war history of Serbian music. Aspiring to discover the archaic musical patterns from the Balkan soil, Ljubica Maric resorted to the collection of Byzantine-Serbian Orthodox liturgical chanting, Octoechos, with its chants divided into eight modes ('voices') according to their melodic patterns and the scales on which they are based. (A similar phenomenon of rediscovering Orthodox music occurred only twenty years later). This collection of Orthodox ecclesiastic chants derived from the Antiochian Octoechos (in use in the Syrian Church since the 6th century), has become the chief musical inspiration of Ljubica Maric. The Octoechos melodies gave rise to the cycle *Music of Octoechos*, including the magnificent *Byzantine Concerto* for piano and orchestra written in 1959. In these works, church melodies are the initial and central subject for incessant variation, whereas the very perspective of the Octoechos, conjoined with the experience of the European musical avant-garde (up to the 50s), gives the style of Ljubica Maric a highly individual profile, and secures its unique place within the whole musical milieu of the 20th century. What often surprises us in the profound and moving emotions expressed in her works (from the late 50s and early 60s) – emotions which somehow encompass the remote regions of our ancestral heritage – is the ways in which they are conveyed; the composer's intuitive gift led her to the anticipation of the repetitive technique, and even to some incipient micropolyphonic elements. It is important to underline that the composer never stopped searching for new dimensions of musical expression. In her superb chamber works created in the 80s and 90s, Ljubica Maric insists on a-thematicism and microtonality in a context, which reduces the tensions and sharpness of her harmonic language. These works invoke the remote regions of renaissance music (through the technique of the Latin organum, for instance), thereby abolishing the exclusivity of the Octoechos, and the whole musical heritage is treated as an archaic frame of reference. Such characteristics bring Ljubica Maric close to postmodernism; yet, she always remains authentic, personal and recognizable in her powerful musical expression.

It seems hardly necessary to mention that the oeuvre of Ljubica Maric was hugely influential in the further development of Serbian music. Turning to musical heritage and regarding it from a modern perspective, appropriate for the times and the sensibility of composers, has become one of the chief lines in Serbian musical creation.

At this same time in the mid-50s, there was another composer who was capable of expressing the unusual originality of his musical talent. Still very young at the time, Dusan Radic (born 1929) surprised Yugoslav audiences by the boldness of his compositions. Starting from a fundamentally pure neo-classicism in the vein of Stravinsky, and building into it elements of folk music, Radic created a particular musical language which can rightly be called – in modern terminology – polystylism. There is no crude pathos in Radic; his music is filled with lucidity and intelligent serenity. These traits are particularly interesting in works which deal with serious events from the Serbian past, such as the cantata *Tower of Skulls* (about the First Serbian Uprising against the Turks). The use of dance-like jazz rhythms in the last movement produces the same striking effect of a pseudo-anachronous fusion of utterly disparate emotional worlds, as does the infernally passionate music of the Nocturnal scene in Schnittke's *Faust-Cantata* – a work that was created 30 years after Radic's. There is no doubt that Radic's compositions from the 50s are among the most original achievements of Serbian music.

In the 1960s belated echoes of serialism were introduced into Serbian music, as well as more recent European developments, like electronics, Ligeti's micropolyphony and aleatory music, whereas the greatest influence came from the Polish composers Lutoslawski and Penderecki. With the exception of two, none of the Serbian composers who assimilated the seductive musical novelties managed to create an authentically individual style; they became imitators instead. The two exceptions, Rudolf Bruci (born 1917) and Ludmila Frajt (1919-1999) superbly combined the experience of Polish music and Ligeti with the tradition of folk music. However, their oeuvre was either relatively modest in size or (in Bruci's case) relatively inconsistent, and they were eclipsed by the prevailing epigonism.

In this musical climate (coinciding with the twenty-year break in the composing career of Ljubica Maric), the sudden bursting onto the scene of Vlastimir Trajkovic (born 1947) in the early 70s was a shock, to say the least. In his extraordinary works of these years Trajkovic dispensed completely with the established mode of expression, introducing, very boldly and consistently, his *non espressivo* style, his music of states rather than changes, giving precedence to simple, pleasing, personal, but not unduly intimate emotions. (His emergence in music was only partly anticipated by his professor, the great Serbian symphonist Vasilije Mokranjac). In order to achieve his particular goal, Trajkovic resorted to minimalism (which, however, he never embraced dogmatically), and to a harmonic language which is close to impressionism. He is not reluctant to make use of jazz or popular music, or to employ melodies from the Balkans. With his subtle use of these musical elements, Trajkovic created an authentic world within a still innocent and not yet abused postmodernism. (One should remember that at the same time, in the early 70s, Arvo Pärt set out on a similar path). Compositions like *Five Nocturnes* for septet, *Duo for Piano and Orchestra* and *Arion* for guitar and string orchestra became cult works in recent Serbian music.

Postmodernism as a complex artistic phenomenon, characterized by the establishment of relations within an overall (in this case) musical heritage, fell on very fertile soil in Serbia. The composers who inclined to neoclassicism and neoromanticism subjected their music to the heterogeneity of postmodernism. It is this in particular which brings out the originality of Zoran Eric (born 1950). His success lies not only in the power of his talent, but also in an adequately chosen medium for which he usually composes: the string orchestra. During the second half of the 20th century the string orchestra was a particularly fruitful field in Serbian music, in view of the number and quality of ensembles as well as of the number and quality of works written for such an ensemble. Zoran Eric's approach to the ensemble has a particular freshness. He generally writes concertos; their sweeping continuous pulse is (neo)baroque in character (sometimes Eric also makes use of Balkan rhythms). He applies repetitive techniques, and jazz and popular music complete the picture. His widely performed works *Cartoon, Off* and *Talea Konzertstück* serve as models to many Serbian composers, and his influence on Serbian music cannot be overestimated.

In the 1990s, political events pushed Serbia into isolation once again. The bad times lasted too long, and the process of recovery is too slow and toilsome, and that has greatly affected the creative spirit. In music, the crisis manifested itself in the domination of some postmodernist slush which embraced the perversities of both vulgar nationalism and the unavoidable classicism and romanticism. Among older composers, only Ljubica Maric stood out through the persevering authenticity of her musical language; a tinge of individuality can to some extent be found in the works of Dejan Despic (born 1930) and Milan Mihajlovic (born 1945).

However, the last decade of the 20th century has also been a time in which new talent has crystallised. The power of the talent possessed by Isidora Zebeljan (born 1967) is reflected primarily in her exceptional predilection for the shaping of melody. Hence the individuality of her musical language. Her compositions furnish proof of the rebirth of melody and harmony; as Kundera would say, the composer 'searches for the melodic truth of the moment'. However, the two components within the music of Isidora Zebeljan mentioned above are completely free of neoromanticism. The expression of her melodies (even when they are close to folk music) belongs primarily to the realm of popular music, which results in a sort of emotional distance, as though contact with the emotions is established trough a crystal mirror. The composer often resorts to the melodic and rhythmic heritage of the Balkan musical tradition (as in *Rukoveti* for Soprano and Orchestra, for instance), but this tradition never assumes the bathos of an awkward past, nor is it a means of investing music with local colour, yet it always bears the marks of freshness and novelty. That is why her compositions seem to originate in the emotional world of contemporary man who is genetically 'aware' of his sonic heritage. This boldness in giving back melody to contemporary man, in authorizing the unrestrained existence of emotions, restores beauty to the music, thus making Isidora Zebeljan one of the most authentic and important bearers of the Serbian music of today.

In this concise survey of Serbian music in the 20th century I have taken into account only the most original authors, only those whose works can be ranked at the top of European musical output. What is remarkable about them is that they all resorted to folk musical traditions in one way or another, in keeping with the individual temperaments of the authors. This should not surprise us. In Serbia folk music is not a museum exhibit; on the contrary, it is very much alive, and its wealth is such that it provides an inexhaustible source of inspiration. However, it is not only the superficial manifestations of folk music that induced composers to address themselves to its treasuries. It is implanted in their genes; it is a vital part of their identities. That is why resorting to one's own musical tradition should be perfectly understandable. Only a handful of them proved capable of passing that collective part of their identity through a personal filter, and their work is the authentic product of someone whose emotions are embodied through the awareness of his or her roots and their ramifications.

Yet, some of you will certainly ask: 'Well, if these composers really are so good, how come I've never heard of them?' It is at this point that the problem of 'small nations' comes in, the problem of 'lateral cultures' or the problem of trend. The political gap within Europe that came about after World War II sharply divided music into Western and Eastern spheres. Serialism flourished in the West, whereas in the East tonality was still the order of the day. (Later on, it was only Polish composers who combined Eastern spirituality with Western rationality). This gap, deepened by the uncompromising repugnance of serialists towards anything which even remotely hinted at tonality, dramatically aggravated the difficulty of presenting contemporary tonal music. How would the expressive world of Ljubica Maric with its blooming modes of Serbian orthodox music have sounded to the ears of avant-gardists during the 1950s? As an anachronism, if indeed it was heard. There were simply no ears sufficiently bold and sober to detect any individual quality in that music, let alone recognize the incipient deviation from avant-gardism. *Byzantine Concerto* which in 1959 announced this deviation definitively and irrevocably, was almost exclusively perceived to be an exotic discovery of the Byzantine world, and was never sufficiently comprehended or accepted in Europe. Sporadic attempts to present Ljubica Maric's unique music to a wider audience (Shostakovich's being the most earnest) ran against obstacles of organization. Dusan Radic's music suffered a similar fate, the more so since his compositions were invariably associated with words, and we know perfectly well what awaits the composer who – to paraphrase Kundera – sacrifices his universal music to an unknown language.

The stylistic dictatorship of Darmstadt over matters of modernism and the avant-garde lasted – though gradually slackening – almost until the beginning of the 1980s. Outside Europe, the mortal blow to its artistic ideology was struck by minimalism, whereas in Europe it was severely upset by Arvo Pärt. And this is what marks the beginning of the breakthrough which brought music back to tonality, and the breakthrough which brought spirituality back to music. This breakthrough is closely related to political changes, that is, with the preparations for the end of communism in Europe and the liberation of non-Russian nations from the confines of the Soviet Union. Hence the enormous support for 'dissident' art, which specifically included a return to religious or ancient folk music. However, why was this very dimension of the oeuvre of Ljubica Maric not discovered at the time? Why did the work of the first Serbian postmodernists Trajkovic and Eric not take off? Unfortunately, an answer to these questions again can only be found in politics. Needless to say, Yugoslavia, which at that time was a country under an extremely liberal socialism, was not perceived to be of 'strategic' importance. In an epoch in which information is disseminated with ever increasing speed, Western listeners and managers (who possess the real economic power), often listen to music with partiality, relying on extra-musical stories. This phenomenon became particularly prominent over the last few years, and it resulted in a considerable chaos in the evaluation of works of art.

But what does the present situation look like, now that the democratization of music enables us to listen to Azeri and Taiwanese classical music? Not very good, as far as Serbia and Serbian music are concerned. I speak from my own experience, as a man who has, over the last ten years, pursued a quixotic campaign of presenting this music. The Balkan wars and political hair-splitting led to a more or less overt discrimination of Serbian culture, with generous help from the mass media. On the other hand, some individuals in the West were willing to peek behind the smoke screen precisely because of the wartime circumstances. Unfortunately, and exactly as in the case of Russian composers – they were more interested in the extra-musical story: this composer was an anti-communist, and that composer supported the unity of Yugoslavia, and a third was a Muslim who lived in Belgrade and consequently suffered, etc. Such attention, although superficially seeming to encourage the presentation of art, actually opposes it, as it does not aim at comprehending the emotional and aesthetic aspects of a work of art. Closely related to this is the so-called phenomenon of discovery. At the core of this phenomenon lies the rather ravenous hunger of established Western musicians, critics and managers to be credited, at all costs, with discovering new, 'spectacular' exponents of Eastern European music (possibly following the example of the Munich-based company ECM). Such 'discoveries' do not bear the slightest resemblance to Sir Charles Mackerras's discovery of Janácek, who meticulously studied his scores, or to the support Boulez gave to Kurtág. The 'discoveries' we have in mind have little to do with the essence of music, and even less with its values. They are generally the manifestation of the musical power-wielders' vanity, who delight in selfishly creating concert seasons, or who rely primarily on verbal concepts and extra-musical contents. In this cage, music that is not enveloped in social-political pathos (and particularly if it comes from the inimical side of recent wars), is hardly given any chance at all.

Under such unpleasant and grave circumstances, the presentation of the highest achievements of Serbian music encounters considerable obstacles. One of the greatest is the chronology of auditory experience. I will remind you of Kundera's idea related to the same problem attendant on Janácek's music: 'Jenufa arrives on world stages twenty years after it was written. Too late. For the polemical character of an aesthetics is lost after twenty years, and it is no longer possible to notice its novelty.'[2] The contemporary Western European listener (and critic as well) has developed the cognition of musical styles to an enviable degree under circumstances secured by concert halls, radio programmes and the jungle of compact discs of our consumer society. With the increase of his knowledge about music, the listener has developed certain categories for classifying this knowledge. Every time he hears some new piece of music, he compares it with a reference from his auditory stock, and afterwards locates the music within his mental compartments. The procedure has become so widespread even among music critics and musicologists, that they often appear not to be able to hear music properly, that what they actually do is scan their 'pigeonholes' trying to find a reference (even a wrong one) to hang on to. If the idea of Orthodox music has been brought to the West by sacred works by Bortnyanski and Rachmaninoff, and was later refreshed by Pärt and Tavener, one wonders how the ear of a Western listener – primed by these authors – will react to an approach to Orthodox music as offered by Ljubica Maric: an approach which has nothing to do with the liturgical act or its imitation? How can one demonstrate the subtle differentiations of the Octoechos modes, when there can be no doubt but that they will invoke wrong associations, or will be perceived as some kind of archaic exoticism? The chronology of the Western

2 *Testaments Betrayed,* p. 191.

perception of new stylistic phenomena is in complete discord with their actual historical origin, and this is what particularly affects the music of Dusan Radic. For, while listening to his polystylistic works, a comparison with Schnittke inevitably imposes itself. The reaction of a Western listener or critic will be something like: we have heard this before, or this is nothing new (in other words, not worthy of attention). And if you try to explain that this tentative polystylism came 30 years before Schnittke's, your collocutor will not believe you, and will sooner doubt your intentions than his or her lack of information.

The music of Vlastimir Trajkovic and Zoran Eric encounters almost the same problem. Regarded from the point of view of the aforesaid chronology of perception, in an indifferent listener and superficial critic they will invoke Pärt or Erkki-Sven Tüür. Inasmuch as Pärt and Tüür are names in which the listener puts his faith, the music of Trajkovic and Eric, despite all their differences, will be compared with the references set by the discographic industry. On the other hand, I often hear a comment that the music of Ljubica Maric is so peculiar that one can hardly put it into any frame of reference. My experience tells me that this comment arises from suspicion; the vanity of the critic will make him wonder how it could be that in 20th-century music something so singular should exist, and yet be unknown to him. The case is similar with Serbian folk music, which a Western European listener usually confuses with Jewish or Gypsy music, as he is unable to distinguish between them.

The last problem I intend to put forward in connection with this is the problem of performance. The performers of contemporary music have undergone a laborious training in order to achieve the technical mastery required to play Darmstadt compositions, not to mention the new complexity. But, their usual manner of performance is still dependent on expressionism. It was the minimalists and Cage and Feldman who broke away from the expressionist tradition of performance, while the music of the so-called mystic minimalists from Eastern Europe often gives rise to romantic performances. What happens, then, with the music of Isidora Zebeljan, which recognizes melody, respects harmony, but whose expression is utterly anti-romantic? The answer is simple: it is romanticized as a rule, since the average musical performer still clings to romantic-expressionist mannerisms, and – except in rare and sporadic cases – has no experience with popular music. Needles to say, an incorrect performance is a prerequisite for incorrect perception (think of the performance of Janácek's music).

In this sea of obstacles, the only true (at least to some degree) way of presenting music is through personal acquaintance. In the case of Serbian music it was only Zoran Eric who managed

to find performers interested in his works, and now they
are performed to considerable acclaim in Great Britain and
Ireland.

And now, I will tell you a nice story about acquaintance and
exceptions. In January 1995 when we organized a concert of
chamber works by Ljubica Maric in Amsterdam's IJsbreker,
Prof. Dr. Marius Flothuis came and, much to our surprise,
inquired about Ms. Maric's health. He told us he had known
about Ljubica Maric since 1933, when her *Wind Quintet*
was performed at the ISCM Festival in Amsterdam. Flothuis
himself did not attend the concert, but afterwards heard from
his colleagues about the extraordinary music of an unknown
Serbian composer (incidentally, critics praised the music).
He remembered the name, and after the war, when he was
art director of the Concertgebouw Orchestra, he tried to find
out about Ljubica Maric. However, apart from hearing one
composition performed at the Warsaw Autumn, Flothuis had
not learned much until 1995. During the last years of his life
he helped us a great deal in presenting the music of Ljubica
Maric, and thanks to him we have found a publisher for her
entire oeuvre, Furore Verlag in Kassel. To quote Kundera one
last time, 'these works, discovered twenty, thirty years after
they had been written, did not have the necessary power to
initiate a movement.'[3]

All in all, the presentation of the music of small nations,
regardless of its value, depends (as it probably always has, for
that matter) on the interest shown by influential producers,
managers and conductors who expect that their promotion will
secure them an important position within the massive global
production of music, which is connected with money – so
obviously the nodal point of our civilization.

Idealism in the presentation of music is old-fashioned and
generally of little consequence. Therefore, I wish we would all
try to contemplate the true essence of music and to approach
it with a pure heart. I am certain that then we shall discover
concealed musical treasuries, and this is part and parcel
of our responsibility towards Music. Thus, we shall greatly
improve our endeavours to make Music (no matter which part
of the planet it comes from) truly accessible to everyone, so
that it may become the undivided heritage of the whole of
humankind. If this is at all possible.

3 *Testaments Betrayed,*
p. 252.

COLOPHON

Editors: Rokus de Groot,
Albert van der Schoot
Authors: Borislav Cicovacki, Peter Davison,
Rokus de Groot, Sander van Maas,
David Matthews, Leo Samama,
Albert van der Schoot, Roger Scruton,
Klaas de Vries
Text-correction: Chris Iles

Design: Kim Broekmeulen & Hanna Donker,
ArtEZ Institute of the Arts Arnhem.
With thanks to Thomas Castro,
Rein Houkes, Joris Maltha

Printing: Veenman Drukkers, Rotterdam

Veenman Publishers
Gijs Stork
Sevillaweg 140
3047 AL Rotterdam
The Netherlands
www.veenmanpublishers.com

ArtEZ Press
Jan Brand, Minke Vos
Postbus 49
6800 AA Arnhem
The Netherlands
www.artez.nl
ArtEZ Press is part of ArtEZ Institute
of the Arts

ISBN/EAN: 978-90-86900-85-5